Keeping Justice

In God's Keeping
Book 1

By

Ronna M. Bacon

Micah 6:8. He has shown you, O man, what *is* good; And what does the Lord require of you but to do justly, To love mercy, And to walk humbly with your God?

Isaiah 30:18. Therefore the Lord will wait, that He may be gracious to you; and therefore He will be exalted, that He may have mercy on you. For the Lord is a God of justice; blessed are all those who wait for Him.

NKJV

Table of Contents

Chapter 1

Raising his face to the sky, Arlyn Koyle closed his gray eyes rapidly. He dropped his head, feeling the pelt of the rain on his dark brown hair. It had not been raining when he set out on his hike. That had moved in over the last thirty minutes. Arlyn was too far away from his truck to run for it. He had to accept the fact that he would be soaked and thoroughly because of the heavy downpour. He looked around for shelter, running towards a strand of trees that he prayed would help. He slid to a stop, looking behind him. Arlyn frowned. Something was bothering him and had been for a few days. Even as he went about his work as an ornithologist, he had felt followed. He had no idea who would be following him.

Walking forward as the rain seemed to slow and almost stop, Arlyn frowned. He should be out here on his own. He just didn't think that he was. Why that was? He had no idea. A whistle broke from his lips as he paced along the path, the whistle that of his favourite hymns. He was out with God that morning, needing the time to be just with his Heavenly Father.

Arlyn frowned once more as he hesitated. Someone was out there and he had no idea if they meant him harm or not. He wasn't picking up on that and he usually did. He frowned deeper, looking for the source of the sound that he had been hearing. It was not the usual sounds of the birds and other creatures and insects.

Walking towards a strand of trees, Arlyn frowned deeper. He felt that was all he was doing that day, frowning and walking towards trees without knowing exactly. He was frustrated as well.

Arlyn paused as he reached the trees, hearing the sound of a female voice. As far as he knew, he was the only one out there. He paused once more, his eyes on the lady in front of him. And it was a lady, he decided, not just a female. There was a gentility about her that cried that she was a lady. He moved to walk towards her, his foot stepping on a fallen twig and it cracked.

The lady jumped and then spun in a circle, trying to determine where the sound had come from. Her blue eyes were huge as she stared towards where Arlyn was still hidden by the trees. Her auburn hair was caught back in a pony tail, the curls showing that she had not been careful with how she was moving.

"Who's there?" Her voice was shaking as she asked her question. She prayed that it was just an animal and not someone sent by her father to track her down and return her to his violent care. She had run the day before, heading out on foot, only what she could carry packed in to the backpack that now rested beside her. She had been desperate to escape him.

Arlyn stepped into what light shone down through the new leaves that had appeared on the trees around them.

"I'm sorry. I didn't mean to scare you." Arlyn kept his voice calm and even. He was surprised, he decided, to find a lady out here.

"Who are you? And why are you out here?" The lady was on her feet, moving back from him. She didn't know him and didn't trust him. She studied him, finding his presence calming.

"I'm sorry, once again. My name is Arlyn Koyle. I'm just out here to enjoy the day. And you would be?" Arlyn's grin widened as he studied her in return.

"I'm Skylor Sage. I don't know where I am. Do you?" Skylor moved back to where her backpack sat, reaching to raise it to her back. She shrugged into the straps.

"I do. You're safe with me, Skylor, if I may call you that." He waited for her nod. "Now, where are you heading? And may I walk with you?" He waited once more for her to speak.

"I have no idea where I am heading. I'm running away and need to keep moving. I don't want to go back to what I left." Skylor drew in a quivering breath, fighting the tears that threatened to overcome her. She didn't think that anyone had been that kind to her all of her life.

"That's okay, Skylor. You're scared and you're running. I don't need to know why. I'll help you." Arlyn reached for her hand. "Come on, Skylor. Let's run away from here. I'll help you." He led her back to the path and then turned back in the direction that he had just come from.

"You want to run away with me? Who says that?" Skylor didn't even bother to try and remove her hand from his. She sensed that he would just not let go of hers. She frowned at that thought. She was not someone that drew protection from anyone. If anything, they turned their backs on Skylor and walked rapidly or ran from her.

Arlyn watched carefully as they walked back towards where he had parked his truck. He felt uneasy but had no idea why. He had never had that feeling before and disliked it very much.

Their steps slowed as they approached the parking lot. Arlyn's eyes were in motion as he searched for anything that he felt was out of the ordinary. He didn't see anything but that didn't mean that there wasn't danger there. He prayed for his new friend and then for himself.

Tucking her into his truck, Arlyn ran around to slid behind the steering wheel. He drove rapidly away from the parking lot, not seeing anyone following them. He kept glancing towards Skylor, not sure what to say to her.

"Skylor? Where would you like to go?" Arlyn pulled his truck into a parking lot and shoved the transmission into park.

"I don't know. I don't want to go home. I have tried for years to get away from the abuse. Last night, I was able to. Now, where would you go if you were me?" Skylor challenged him and then sighed. "I'm sorry. I shouldn't have said that."

"It's okay. I don't know where I would go. Listen, I have an apartment in the basement of my house. It's empty. You're welcome to use it until you decide what you want to do." Arlyn began to pray for the lady with him.

"You would do that? You don't know me." Skylor felt the first glimmer of hope that she had ever felt. "Why?"

"Why? Why would I do this?" At her nod, Arlyn drew in a deep breath. He could not tell her that he didn't want to see her walk away from him, not then, not ever. "It's what I do, Skylor. I try to be the hands and feet of God on earth. This is one way that I can do that. The apartment is used for emergency purposes or to house people who speak or work at our church for short term. I would be happy to have you as a neighbour." He grinned at her before he gave a shout and shot out of the parking lot. He watched the truck following him. It was a much bigger truck than his and whoever was driving it didn't mean to approach them for their health,

Skylor screamed as she reached to grip whatever it was that she could. She didn't understand what had just happened.

"Arlyn? Did you really have to do that?" The anger in her voice lashed at him.

"I did. There's a truck following us. And I don't think that they want us to stop and be friendly with them. That's not how I'm reading this situation." He shot her a quick glance. "Skylor. Talk to me. Tell me why you ran and who is chasing you."

"How do you know that they are after me? They could be after you." Skylor refused to speak, knowing

———

11

that if she did, Arlyn would just drop her on the side of the road and drive away.

Arlyn squinted against the shafts of the late afternoon sun that cut through the trees and buildings. He had no idea what was going on but he was determined to protect this lady.

"They could be but once more, Skylor. Talk to me." Arlyn could feel himself growing angry, not at her but at the situation that he found himself in.

"I don't know. I have had no freedom my whole life. My father kept me hidden and a captive. He was physically abusive and was also emotionally abusive. I finally had the opportunity to run last night and just did. I had walked to where you found me. He's not going to let me go. I don't understand why." Skylor swiped at the tears on her face, a scream coming from her as the truck behind them rammed Arlyn's truck.

Arlyn struggled to control his truck, not wanting to crash while in town. And he was not prepared to drive outside of town. A second ram from behind sent his truck skittering across the road and towards a small building. He drew in a deep breath and began to pray. He could not stop the truck.

The truck slammed into the building and through it. The sudden stop of the truck sent both Arlyn and Skylor flying forward and then back. They both lay still, not seeing the man from behind them walk towards Arlyn's truck and then with an evil smile on his face drive away.

Chapter 2

Shouts sounded through the stillness that ensued after the sounds of the crash died down. Men ran towards the building, finding it collapsed on top of the truck, trapping whoever was inside. They could not see into the cab. Speculation as to the cause was tossed around, including that the driver was drunk. Red and blue emergency lights lit up the sky as police, fire, and paramedic services appeared. The spectators grew, murmuring among themselves.

One police officer paused as he saw the plate and stared at it. He shook his head as an officer asked if he thought the driver was drunk.

"It's Arlyn Koyle's truck. There is no way that he would have been drinking." Joe reached to help with the debris.

The truck finally cleared of as much debris as was possible for the emergency personnel to access the truck cab. Firefighters dragged the equipment that was needed to pry open the doors before the paramedics reached to assess the couple inside.

Joe walked towards the cab, standing back where he could watch the activity inside. He frowned as he saw the lady in the passenger's seat. He didn't know her but would certainly questioning her and also Arlyn.

Arlyn's body had slumped as far forward over the steering wheel as the seat belt would allow him. The paramedics worked carefully to assess him before one of them reached for a neck collar to stabilize his head and neck before they moved him backwards onto the seat. The paramedics' gaze shifted to where another pair of paramedics was assessing Skylor.

Moving the two to backboards and then stretchers, the paramedics shoved the stretchers towards the rigs and then disappeared. Joe watched them go and then turned back to his investigation. It troubled him that a friend had been involved in such an accident but to have a lady involved as well was troubling, He reached for his phone, knowing that he had to call Arlyn's family and not wanting to do that. Joe's thoughts were troubled. He wasn't sure which of Arlyn's family to call. Arlyn's brother, Briar, won the mental toss as to which family member would be called.

"Hello?" Briar's voice sounded across the air waves.

"Briar? It's Joe?" Joe hesitated to speak. "Where are you?"

"At home. Why?" Briar had a sudden sensation that something was wrong with one of his brothers. "Which one?"

"Arlyn. He crashed his truck into a building at the edge of town. And no, I don't know why." Joe frowned at the scene, watching as evidence was collected and the way cleared for the tow truck to hook up Arlyn's truck to take it to the police garage. "Was Arlyn dating? I hadn't heard that he was."

"No, he wasn't. Why would you ask that?" Briar locked his house door behind him and ran for his truck.

—

"There was a lady in his truck. She's unconscious as well. I just wondered if he had suddenly found a lady. Head off for the hospital, Briar. You're calling Cayce?" Joe thought that he would but had to ask.

"I will. Thanks, Joe. Catch up with me when you can." Briar clicked off from that call before he just sat, not sure what had been going on with Arlyn. What had happened was totally not Arlyn. He was one of the most cautious and careful drivers that Briar knew. He sighed as he reached for his phone, intent on calling his brother.

"Cayce?" Briar could hear the music in the background and the slight sound of plates and utensils being set on a table. "You're at home?"

"I am, Briar. Are you on your way?" Cayce grinned as he contemplated his table. The three brothers had planned to meet for a meal. Their bond was strong, being triplets. Arlyn was the oldest, Cayce the youngest.

"Put your meal away, Cayce, and head for the hospital. Arlyn's been in a truck accident. Joe just called me. And I don't have any more information than that. Other than there was a lady in the cab with Arlyn."

Cayce listened with horror to his brother's words before he was setting away the meal and then running for his truck.

"A lady? Did you really say a lady?" Cayce's truck shot out of the driveway as he headed for the hospital.

"I did. At least, that's what Joe said. He's meeting us there." Briar found a parking spot and ran for the Emergency Department. He sighed to himself as he was told to find a seat and that they would call him in when they could. He didn't know what they would be facing with Arlyn but he knew that God was in control and would provide the answers that they needed.

Briar turned as he felt a hand on his shoulder. Cayce stood there, a puzzled and worried look on his face.

"Briar? Any word?" Cayce looked around before he drew Briar to seats near the entrance.

"No, not yet. They'll call us when they're ready for us." Briar's hands drew down his face. "I'm worried, Cayce. What happened to him?"

Both brothers could feel Arlyn's pain to some extent. It was how it was with them.

"I don't know, Briar. Wasn't he going hiking today?" Cayce was thinking through the conversation that the brothers had had the night before.

"He was. I don't know where he came from. Joe didn't say much and I wish that he had." Briar's eyes closed as he struggled with his emotions. Nothing like this had ever happened to the brothers. "Mom and Dad?"

Cayce shook his head. Their parents were on a cruise ship somewhere near Alaska, a dream trip that had finally been achieved.

"We'll reach out once we hear how Arlyn is. I just wish they would hurry up." Cayce looked up as he hard footsteps heading their way.

Joe slowed his footsteps as he approached the brothers. He was not sure what he could tell them. There was not a lot of evidence. The mechanic had pointed at the tailgate and the box of the truck. The large dent was evident that something dire had happened to Arlyn. They would need to speak with him but the physician had simply shaken his head. He had no idea when that would be possible.

Briar and Cayce shared a look before looking back at Joe as he sat beside them. They weren't sure what to ask. All they knew was that their big brother was injured and they hadn't seen him as yet to reassure themselves that he was okay.

"He's still unconscious, guys." Joe drew in a deep breath. "And I can tell you that this was a deliberate act against him. We just don't understand why."

Chapter 3

Cayce stared at Joe before he stared at the door to the examination rooms. He wanted to be through that door and with his brother, to fully understand what had happened. That wasn't possible at the moment. The brothers needed to wait and that was a difficult task to do.

Joe rose at last, heading back to find the physicians treating the couple. He didn't understand how Skylor came to be there. She was hours away from her family and home town. He hadn't reached out to her family as yet, not knowing why she was in their town of Grasspoint.

The physician treating Skylor looked around as Joe appeared. His attention went back to Skylor as he continued to assess her injuries.

"How is she, Doc?" Joe spoke at last.

"She's not as injured as I originally thought. No broken bones. Some soft tissue injuries. A possible concussion. Do we know anything about her?"

"No, we don't." Joe was honest with the physician. "She's not from here. I haven't reached out to her folks yet. I want to speak with her first."

The physician nodded, knowing how Joe worked. They had met many times in just such a way.

"I see. Arlyn's brothers are here?"

"They are. Their parents are away on a dream cruise. They won't call them until they've spoken with

Arlyn." Joe walked away to enter the room where Arlyn was.

Arlyn had roused, not sure where he was or why. He had become somewhat combative, unusual for him. He was usually a serene and calm person.

"I want up." Arlyn kept shoving at the hands holding him down. "Let me up."

Joe appeared in his line of sight, causing Arlyn to frown at him.

"Joe? Why won't they let me up? What happened?" Arlyn was still struggling to rise.

"Lie still, Arlyn. You were in an accident and unconscious when you were found. I need to speak with you. I can't do that if you won't be still." Joe's voice was stern as he spoke with Arlyn.

Arlyn finally rested back on the stretcher, not taking his eyes from Joe.

"Explain yourself, Joe. And now." Arlyn's words were spit at Joe, not his usual way of speaking.

"I will." Joe watched as the medical personnel disappeared. "Talk to me, Arlyn. What happened today? It's not you to crash your truck."

Arlyn sighed. No, it was not him to do that. This time? He had had no control over what had happened and he told Joe as much. He went back over the day, a frown on his face as he talked about the lady who he had found.

"Skylor? Where is she?" Arlyn was off the stretcher and searching for the lady. He found her, a hand reaching to rest on her hair. He was surprised to find her turning into his hand. He bit at his lip, knowing that his brothers were likely waiting for him, but Arlyn knew that he could not walk away from the lady. She was in danger, he decided, and God had told him to help her. Even though the words were not audible, Arlyn knew what he had to do. He would not turn his back on her.

"Come on, Arlyn. Let's find your brothers." Joe watched in silence as Arlyn shook his head. "Arlyn? What's her story?"

"Skylor? She's on the run from an abusive parent. I got that much information from her. I need to find somewhere for her to stay." He looked around. "Our backpacks?"

"I have them. Let's find your brothers and reassure them that you're fine. Then, we'll look for somewhere for Skylor." Joe waited for Arlyn to speak. "Arlyn? What happened?"

"It was bizarre. I found Skylor out on the trail that I wanted to walk today. We had to hide for a few moments when two men appeared. I drove away from there and was heading for my home. I didn't see the truck. It just rammed me from behind and I lost control. I didn't have a chance to react, Joe, and that's not me." Arlyn was distraught at that and then very worried about the lady who had dropped into his life.

"We didn't thank that you had much of a chance to respond. Do you know that you drove into a building?" Joe watched Arlyn as his head shot around and then his eyes closed.

"A building? I drove into a building? It came down on the truck?" Arlyn waited for Joe to speak.

"It did. Not totally but enough that it damaged your truck. You'll need to find another one. And it's in the police garage right now so that we can go over it." Joe smiled in sympathy at Arlyn shook his head. "We'll get you in to get your gear from it. Your brothers have your backpack as well as the one belongs to this lady. What do you know about her?"

Arlyn drew in a deep breath. He prayed for the lady who shared the adventure with him. He felt unsafe and didn't know if it was because of him or her.

"Not a lot, Joe. Not a lot. I know her name and where she's from. I also know that she is on the run from an abusive father. She mentioned physical and emotional abuse. We'll need to find her someone to talk to. But first, we need to find somewhere for her to say. I had offered her the apartment. We hadn't come to an agreement on that as of yet." Arlyn kept his eyes on Skylor. "She's not going anywhere any time soon."

"No, she's not. Now, you need to find your brothers. They are beyond worried about you. If they could, they would have worn a path into the tiled floor out there." Joe jerked his thumb towards the waiting room. "For now, Arlyn, I'll have the hospital put down the apartment address and your phone number on Skylor's chart. And you can be her contact person. For now, Arlyn. Just for now. She needs someone in her corner in this town. You have that connection with her that we don't. Come on, my friend. You'll get to come back and find her again." Joe's hand on Arlyn's

---

shoulder directed his friend away from Skylor and towards his brothers.

"I don't know that I want to see them." Arlyn's steps slowed as he approached the door to the waiting room. "Do I really have to go out there?"

Joe began to laugh. Arlyn was the oldest of the triplets, older that Briar by fifteen minutes and older than Cayce by twenty-five minutes. They were the anomaly in their small town, the only triplets in town. They were also very protective of one another. Hurt one of them? You hurt all three. Joe had seen them defend one another far too many times over the years. He had been a schoolmate of theirs and also a close friend.

"You do need to see them. And they need to see you. I've reached out to your Dad. They're stuck on the cruise ship for now. He said that if you really needed him, they would find a way to fly home."

"No, I don't think that I do. I don't want them to cut their dream vacation short. Not when I'm still on my feet and relatively unscathed." Arlyn shoved open the door and stepped through, searching for his brothers. He walked towards them, finding them on their feet approaching him.

Joe watched as the brothers hugged one another and then found chairs. He gave an amused sound as he saw that Arlyn had chosen a seat where he could watch the door. Arlyn had a connection with Skylor that was not seen often with strangers. And Joe shivered, feeling afraid for his friend. All he could do was pray for him and Skylor.

Chapter 4

Cayce kept glancing at his brother, not sure whether to speak or what even to ask him. He shared a look with Briar who shrugged. Both of them had been praying for their brother.

"Arlyn? What happened?" Briar finally broke through the silence that they were sitting in.

Arlyn shrugged. He was not sure what had exactly happened and said as much.

"Who's the lady?" Cayce was puzzled by that. His brother was not dating, not that they knew about.

"Skylor? Her name is Skylor Sage. She was just out there on her own. She had been walking from her home town, running away from an abusive father." Arlyn's face darkened at that thought. "We were heading back here and had to hide for a bit. Two men showed up on the trail. I don't know who they were looking for." He sighed. "And you know what happened when I hit the edge of town. Before you ask, I didn't see the truck. I guess my attention was on Skylor and trying to determine how we can help her."

"The apartment." Cayce spoke for himself and Briar.

"I offered it to her. She hadn't said that she would take it. I was going to show it to her and then let her make up her mind. If she didn't want it, I would have found somewhere for her to stay." Arlyn drew in a deep breath, knowing that he would not walk away

———

from the lady who God had brought into his life. "I can't walk away from her, guys. You both know that."

"We know that, Arlyn. We support you in that decision. How is she?"

Arlyn shrugged, on his feet as he saw the nurse looking for him. He followed her, leaving silence in his wake. His brothers shared a look and then both shrugged, settling back on their chairs, content to wait for Arlyn no matter how long it took.

Skylor looked up in fear as she heard the footsteps approaching her bed. She didn't think that they sounded like her father's but she knew that no man would ever help her. Not unless it was the man named Arlyn who had helped her earlier. And she just knew that he had disappeared. She had begged God for years for help. Only that never happened.

Arlyn paused beside the bed, a hand reaching out to still the one that was picking at the blanket. Skylor stared up at Arlyn, surprised to see him and then happy that he had not walked away from her.

"Skylor?" Arlyn didn't know what to ask. He wanted to hear that she was okay but he really didn't think that she was.

"Arlyn? Where are we? What happened?" Skylor surprised both of them by launching herself at him.

Arlyn caught her, wrapping her into a hug. He had not expected her to do that. He stared down at the auburn head buried against him. He gave a shrug, just knowing that he would stay near her to protect her.

———

"We were in an accident, Skylor. And you are in our local hospital. I think that you can leave. Only I have no idea where you're going to go." Arlyn was distressed at that.

"I don't know, Arlyn." Skylor shoved away from him. "You had an apartment?"

"I do. And you can use it for however long you need to. There is no rent." Arlyn studied her once more, seeing the surprise on her face. "Yes, you heard me right. I don't charge rent for it."

Skylor shrugged. If that was how Arlyn wanted to do it, that was his decision. She slid from the bed, staring at Arlyn's hand that he was holding out for her. She stared up at him, finding him just giving a shrug, a grin on his face. She shrugged herself and reached for it, feeling the strength of character that came through. She wondered if God was doing this, providing someone to protect her from her father and whoever it was that he worked for.

"Okay, Skylor?" Arlyn waited patiently for Skylor to nod. "Okay. Let's get you home. We'll stop and find some groceries for you, at least until tomorrow."

"But your truck? Is it here?" Skylor looked up at him once more. She didn't see the two men who looked so much like Arlyn stopping nearby, watching their brother and the lady with him.

"No, it's at the police garage. My brothers are here. They'll give us a lift. You'll be tired of seeing them." He pointed in front of them. "The one on the left is Briar. The other one is Cayce."

Skylor stared at the two men before her head swung around so that she could study Arlyn. Her head swung back and forth a number of times before Briar took pity on her.

"We're triplets, Skylor, if I may call you that. Arlyn in the oldest, I'm next, and Cayce is the youngest." He grinned at her. "Does that explain why we look so much alike?"

"It does. I've never met triplets before." Skylor sighed. "I haven't even met twins. My father wouldn't let me out of the house no matter how much I begged to go out. He made me home school even up to high school graduation. Can you help me find out why?"

"We can do that, Skylor. In fact, we will start working on that tomorrow." Cayce's hand went up. "We know. It's Sunday but that won't make any difference. We'll escort you and Arlyn to church and then back to his home for lunch. We'll provide that. For now, let's get you and Arlyn home. I'll make a food run for you. Do you have any preferences?"

Skylor stared at him before her gaze turned to Briar who was nodding and then to Arlyn, who was also nodding, a look on his face that said he would do all he could in his power to protect her.

"What are we protecting you from, Skylor? Or are we protecting Arlyn?" Cayce was puzzled at that. He didn't think that they had enough information to determine that.

"I don't know, Cayce." Arlyn didn't look away from Skylor. "We don't know for sure, do we?"

Skylor shifted on her feet, not sure where to go or who to look at. She was at a loss as to where to go. She sensed that God was there in the room with them. She could feel His presence. Skylor was not used to being around people, especially men who seemed to care what happened to her and wanted her to express her wishes.

"Skylor?" Briar's voice cut through her thoughts, causing her to turn to him. "Are you ready to leave?"

Skylor nodded, her eyes on Arlyn. She stared at the hand that he was stretching out for her to take. She frowned at it and then up at him. He simply grinned at her and continued to wait patiently for Skylor to respond. He prayed for the new lady in his life, begging God for protection for her. He was not convinced that it was her father who had sent those men. He just wasn't sure. They could have been after him, just as easily, he decided.

Reaching tentatively for Arlyn's hand, Skylor felt it close over her hand in a warm and welcoming grasp. She rightly read him that he would protect her. She just wasn't used to a man doing that for her. Her experience had been that men would hurt her.

Chapter 5

Skylor didn't move from where she stood just inside the apartment door. She was afraid to, she decided, and didn't know why. Cayce had appeared with bags of food that he was sorting out into the cupboards and fridge and freezer. He kept shooting glances at her. He wasn't sure why she had not moved. Cayce was also certain that Briar had been followed from the hospital. He had been behind him for a bit and a car had cut inbetween them before he headed off towards the grocery store.

Briar had walked through the apartment, trying to see it from Skylor's point of view and not able to. He returned to stand where he could watch Arlyn and Skylor. A small smile crossed his face before he shook his head.

"Skylor? What's wrong?" Arlyn was at a loss to know how to proceed. He usually avoided the ladies, if he could.

Skylor shrugged. She wasn't sure what was wrong. She just didn't know.

"I don't know, Arlyn." She looked up at him, a lost little girl look on her face. "I've never been on my own before. Not once in my life. My father made sure that if he was ever away, someone was in the house." She drew in a shaky breath, her suppressed sobs obvious to the three men. "I'm afraid, Arlyn. Does that make sense?"

"It does, Skylor. It does." Arlyn shared a look with his brothers, trying to think of a lady who could come and stay the night with her. "If I can find a lady to stay with you tonight, would that work?"

Skylor stared at him, first in shock and then in wonder. No one had ever offered her that before.

"You would do that? You don't know me."

"No, we don't, Skylor." Briar walked towards her, a hand resting gently on her shoulder for a moment. His heart broke as he felt her flinch and then removed his hand quickly. "You're a lady who needs someone with her. We can't do that but we know someone who would." He walked away to the outdoors, looking up at the dusky sky and pulled out his phone. He dialled a number, waiting patiently for the lady to answer. "Aunt Anna? Are you around?"

"I am, Briar. Why? What's this I hear about Arlyn? He needs my help." Anna Koyle reached for her purse and the small bag that she had packed earlier that day at God's prompting.

"Not Arlyn in particular. He's off on an adventure of some kind. There's a lady involved." Briar grinned at her snort. She was his father's younger sister, young enough that she still joined in their activities but old enough to know when to step back.

"Of course there is. Where is she?" Anna shut her car door and drove away from her home, heading for Arlyn. She prayed for her nephew and then for the lady involved. She didn't need to know much more than what Briar had told her.

—

"She's in the apartment but is afraid. The thing of it is, Aunt Anna, is that she has been abused all of her life and has had no freedom. She has freely admitted that and she really doesn't know what to do."

Anna's heart broke at the news. She worked with abuse victims and was just the person who was needed.

"I'm almost there. Do I need to pick up anything?"

"No, Cayce did a food run." Briar bit at his lip. "I just don't know about clothing and all that stuff, Aunt Anna."

"It's okay. I'll stop somewhere and find some things that will get her by for the next day or so until we ascertain exactly what is needed." She dropped her phone back into her purse before she shot off onto another route and to a friend's store. Shopping quickly, she was back in her car and heading for Arlyn's.

Arlyn looked up as the door opened and he drew in a sigh of relief. Skylor had not moved from where she had stopped.

Anna looked between her nephew and the lady before she just reached to hug Skylor. She felt Skylor stiffen before she relaxed in the hug. Anna knew at that point that Skylor not likely had had many hugs in her life and was determined to change that.

"Skylor?" Anna waited patiently for Skylor to look at her. She stood with an arm around the younger lady. "I am aunt to these three boys. They reached out to me, knowing that you needed someone with you tonight. Is that correct?"

Skylor stared at the older lady, not sure what was happening. She felt safe with the lady and wondered at that. Her gaze turned to Arlyn, finding him smiling at her and nodding.

"You do need someone with you, Skylor. Aunt Anna is perfect for that." Arlyn walked away not that much later, heading for his own home and his bed. He was hurting more than he had ever imagined that he could ever hurt.

Briar and Cayce shared a look before they followed their brother. Something was going on with him and they didn't want to miss out on it. Darkness soon covered the house as the lights went out one by one. No one heard the activity outside of it over the night as the men tried to find a way in and couldn't. Arlyn's house was just not that accessible to those who wanted to bring harm to him and harm to the lady who now resided in the basement apartment.

Joe approached the house the next morning, frowning. A neighbour had reported activity outside of the house overnight and he could not ignore it. He tapped at Arlyn's front door, not surprised to have Anna answer it.

"Anna? You're here? Of course you are." Joe hugged her before he walked towards the kitchen.

Skylor turned as she heard new footsteps and froze. She didn't know the police officer. Her contact with the police had been that of threats. Skylor backed away and backed into Arlyn, not realizing that he was standing right behind her. She felt his arms around her and jumped, not sure of his intentions.

"Skylor? How are you this fine morning?" Joe grinned at her before he sobered. "Arlyn, do you know that men were outside of your home last night, trying to gain access to it?"

Arlyn sobered, the grin wiped from his face.

"How many?"

"At least three that we can see. Your neighbour called it in. You didn't hear anything?" Joe's voice was stern as he spoke.

Arlyn stared at the framed photos on the wall, pictures of his favourite birds.

"I didn't hear anything. And neither Briar or Cayce mentioned anything." He sighed. "We're off on that adventure, are we, Joe?"

"I would suspect so. Now, we need to talk and talk hard, Arlyn. Someone is after either you or Skylor. I want to know who and why." Joe gave a smile at Skylor that didn't relax her in any way. "Skylor?"

"I need to leave." She struggled to escape Arlyn's arm, a sob rising within her. Arlyn just didn't let her go.

"It's okay, Skylor. It's okay." He kept his voice low and soothing. "It's okay." Arlyn hugged her tighter even though she fought him. "We'll figure it out. For now, let's sit and have the breakfast that you and Anna made. Then, we'll pray this through. God is here. He doesn't leave us or forsake us. He is in

---

control. Just remember that you were prayed for in the garden. And all you need to do is reach out for the hem of that garment for healing."

Chapter 6

Late that morning, Skylor turned from the dresser in her room. Anna had been out and back with more clothes and whatnot for her. Skylor had tried to refuse but Anna had simply hugged her and then sent her to put the clothes and everything else away. She turned to study the bedroom before moving to the bathroom. It was luxury, Skylor decided, luxury that she had never experienced before.

Anna was waiting for her as she walked through the living room, a smile on her face. Anna was troubled about her young friend, just not sure how to get her to open up about her life. That would come, she knew, as trust developed. And Anna was impatient for that trust to develop. She was worried about her nephew and the danger that he was in. Arlyn didn't need to say much. Anna had been around too many people in danger not to understand the signs.

"Skylor? What would you like to do? I know it's too late for church but we could do our own." Anna grinned at her, suddenly looking as young as her nephews.

"We could? I've never been inside a church building, Anna. I wasn't allowed. I'm sorry that you missed it this morning." Skylor's face was shuttered, something that she had learned very early to do. If she showed any emotions, no matter how minor, she was severely punished for that.

"It's okay, Skylor. I don't always get there. They do a live stream that we can watch if you would rather."

"They do? I've never seen a live stream. How does it work?" Skylor walked into Anna's hug before she stepped back.

"We do this." Anna connected her laptop to the television set and quickly found the live stream. She settled back on the couch, watching Skylor as she did so.

Skylor's attention was on the television. She was in awe that something like this existed. She knew nothing about electronics or computers but she was determined to learn and learn quickly. She was so engrossed in studying the electronics and then listening to the service that she didn't hear Anna arise and walk to the door, opening it to allow Arlyn, Briar, and Cayce to enter. Joe almost ran towards the door, grinning at Anna as he did so.

Anna turned to watch her nephews, a frown in place. They were joking among themselves as usual but she could see the sternness and soberness in Arlyn, something that she didn't think that she had seen before. She nodded and then prayed for her nephew and his lady. God would need to stand in front of them to protect them. Of that, she was convinced.

Arlyn turned to find Skylor, worried about her. He had been out that morning, Sunday and all, and purchased a cell phone for her, just adding it to his own plan. He had programmed in every number that he could think of. Arlyn highly doubted that Skylor had a phone, given how she had described her life

Sitting beside her, Arlyn waited for Skylor to acknowledge that he was there. A slight smile of amusement as he watched her face. He saw as she turned her face to him and then back to the television. He patiently waited for her to turn back to him.

Skylor jumped as she realized that someone was sitting beside her. She spun on the couch and stared at Arlyn.

"Where did you come from?" Her voice rose to a squeak by the end of her question

"From my house?" Arlyn grinned at her. "You were engrossed in the service."

"I was. I've never been to church. I was never allowed to. Anna found this for me." Skylor didn't look distressed or sad, just resigned to what her life had been.

"You haven't? We'll change that." Arlyn hesitated for a moment. "You slept okay?"

"I did, the best sleep that I think I have had. All my life I have had broken sleep. My father didn't think anything about waking me up to emotionally abuse me or to even physically hit me during the night." She shrugged, not realizing the concern that flooded the five listening to her.

"He did that?" Arlyn wrapped an arm around her and hugged her, not finding that she responded at all. He hadn't expected her to. He began to pray for her, causing her to turn to watch him before her eyes closed and a single tear trickled down her face.

"Thank you, Arlyn." Skylor moved away from him, her eyes back on the television and the end of the service. She sighed. She had no idea how to react or what to say. This was beyond the scope of what she had ever encountered. She prayed for herself at last, never having done that before. She had just begged God to release her from her situation. That had not happened until then. "Why now, Arlyn? How did I manage to escape?"

Arlyn nodded as he watched Joe approach and sit beside her on the other end of the couch.

"I don't know, Skylor. It seems as if God has managed that for you. We forget that what we go through is at His will and timing. He has allowed the life you lived for a reason. He also freed you at this time for His own purpose."

Skylor had turned to face Joe, frowning at him. She saw the compassion on his face.

"Joe? What do you want?" She was grumpy and refused to apologize for it.

"What do I want? Today? I'm here as a friend. Tomorrow, I'll be here as a police officer." He grinned at her. "I will talk with you more about your family and your father, Skylor. I've already done that with Arlyn, although because we're friends, I don't have to ask too many questions."

"A friend? Is that what you are?" Skylor waited for him to nod. "I've never had any friends before, do you know that?" She turned her head as she heard Arlyn's angry growl. "Arlyn? I can't change that. No one can. It is what it is." She was on her feet, walking towards the kitchen, ignoring Briar and Cayce. She reached into the fridge for a bottle of water, turning it around in her hand. This was also something new for her, being able to choose what she wanted to drink and when.

Anna stood with a hand over her mouth before she stepped outside of the house. Her emotions were just too high. She stared around the yard before she marched across the yard to the side of the yard. She frowned at the box sitting there before she marched back to the apartment door, opened it and called for Joe.

Joe appeared in an instant, worried at the tone of voice that Anna was using. It was not normal for her.

"Anna? What's wrong?"

"Come with me." Anna marched back across the yard and pointed at the box. "That doesn't belong here. I didn't touch it. You need to look after it." She moved back to the patio outside of the apartment, wrapping an arm around Skylor, the triplets gathering behind them. Arlyn stood with his hands on Skylor's shoulders. That lady didn't move from under his touch.

"What happened, Aunt Anna?" Briar finally asked the question that had been burning in all of them.

"I found a box over there. It doesn't belong and it was not there last night. I know that. I walked the yard early this morning." Anna was angry, more angry than she had ever been. "Who did this? And which one of you are they after?"

Arlyn shrugged, not sure what to say. He shared a look with his brothers before he moved around the ladies and walked slowly towards Joe who was standing in the centre of the yard.

"Joe? What's that?" Arlyn waited patiently for Joe to speak. Patience was something that he usually had an abundance of. This time, that patience was in short supply.

"That box is what is going on. And I have no idea what it is. I've called it in, including the bomb squad. We don't know who put it there. It would be out of sight of your security cameras." Joe had already determined that.

"Then, more go up. I'll pick them up after work tomorrow." Arlyn sighed, his hands dragging down his face. "How do I go to work and leave Skylor on her own? We all have to work."

"Can you take her with you? Are you out in the field or in the office? And you did say that you needed help in the office, didn't you?" Joe gave a grim smile as he asked that, hearing the sounds of car door closing and knowing that help had arrived.

"I'm in the office, and yes, I do need help. She's never worked, you know, Joe. She was kept hidden away. And I want to know why." Arlyn felt the anger rising inside him and then prayed for that anger to disappear.

—

Chapter 7

Joe walked slowly back towards the house. He knew that the group was now in Arlyn's portion of the house, likely working on a meal that no one wanted to eat. He sighed. The box had not held a bomb, which was a relief. But the contents puzzled him. Joe was not sure which one of the couple that it was directed to. He suspected Arlyn but would not be surprised to find that it was Skylor.

"Joe? What was in the box?" Arlyn stopped in front of him, not letting him pass him.

"Arlyn? The box? Is that what you mean?" Joe watched as Arlyn nodded. "There was only a photo of you two from the trail. Someone was following you that day. Following you and not Skylor. Do you understand that?"

Arlyn nodded. It was about what he expected.

"Why would someone be tracking you, Arlyn? What about you would cause that?" Joe had no idea where this investigation would be leading.

"I have no idea." Arlyn rubbed at the back of his neck. "I wonder."

"You wonder what?" Joe pressed Arlyn on his thoughts, unsure what Arlyn was not stating.

"The birds. There is a black market for birds. Is someone after me for that?" Arlyn turned as he felt someone beside him. Skylor was there, her hand on his back. She had managed to gather enough courage to approach him. "Skylor?"

"Arlyn? What was in the box? There must have been something."

"There was, Skylor. A photo of you and Arlyn on the trail." Joe was frustrated at that.

"A photo? Who did that?" Skylor stretched up on her toes to study the photo that Joe was holding out for her. "I don't know why they would do. I don't know anyone here. Not at that point other than Arlyn."

"We know that, Skylor. We do know that. Now, we just have to figure out why and who." He watched as she walked back towards the house where Anna, Briar and Cayce were waiting for her. She simply walked past the trio and into the apartment, the door closing quietly behind her.

"Arlyn? Is she okay?" Joe was beginning to worry about her.

"I have no idea, Joe. She's shuttered herself once more. It will take time. I know that you will be investigating her. Just be cautious with her. That's all I ask. She's been driven down so much all of her life, I don't know that she'll ever recover." Arlyn walked back towards his family, pausing to speak with them before he tapped at the apartment door and waited for Skylor to open it. He walked into the apartment, the door staying open.

Skylor turned to watch Arlyn, seeing the compassion on his face. She frowned at him. She was not used to that, the hatred spewed towards her more common that kindness.

"Arlyn? What do we do?" Skylor sighed. "Where is God in all this?"

"He's right here, Skylor. He is right here. He is in the midst of everything we are going through. I just wish that it was different. I want to help you, Skylor, if you'll let me."

Skylor studied him and sighed. He was taking over, wasn't he? And she would just let him. She had no fortitude to withstand him. And suddenly, Skylor didn't want to. She welcomed him to do just that. She had never had a knight in her life to stand in front of her.

"You want to do that?" Skylor's voice was almost inaudible.

"I do. And so do my family. And I know that my friends will step in and help." He pointed behind him, a grin on his face. "And Joe will come back and speak with you many times. He does that until he understands what he needs to and he has the information that he has to have. We'll not leave you, Skylor. Never."

Skylor nodded slowly. It was about what she expected him to say, what little that she knew of him. She turned to stare out of the door, moving at last to stand beside Anna. She could hear Arlyn's footsteps behind her and jumped slightly as his hands rested on her shoulders. Skylor didn't know what to think. This caring and compassion was beyond what she had ever experienced in her life.

The next morning, Arlyn found himself just standing in his office, staring down at his desk. He had no desire to be there. Instead, he wanted to be where Skylor was. That lady was with his aunt, out and about somewhere. He worried about Skylor without knowing exactly why.

Delving into his work, Arlyn looked up at last. He had worked through all that he needed to and rose, heading for the outdoors and then for a walk around his neighbourhood. He needed to be out in the outdoors and hopefully clear his head. He watched as he returned to his home, frowning. Something was off but he just didn't know what. Arlyn sighed as he began a systematic search, not finding anything. Heading inside, he reached for his home computer and pulled up the security video feed. There was nothing out of the ordinary that he could see. He still felt something was off. He just didn't know what.

Listening carefully, he heard the soft sounds from his back deck and headed that way, stopping to grab two bottles of juice from the fridge. He stepped outside, startling Skylor.

"I'm sorry. I'll leave." Skylor started to rise from the glider before she sat back at Arlyn's nod.

"It's okay, Skylor. You're more than welcome to use the back deck and the front deck as well. Here." Arlyn handed over the bottle of juice before he carefully sat beside her, his motions slow and careful.

"I can? I'm not used to that, you do know that?" Skylor frowned at him, feeling a further freeing of her heart and life.

―

43

"I do know that, Skylor. Tell me about your day." Arlyn sat back and watched her face, seeing the conflicting emotions chasing across her face.

"Your aunt is just so wonderful. She should have been working today, she said, but took it off to spend with me. She shouldn't have done that." Skylor was distressed at that.

"It's who she is, Skylor. You needed her today. And she needed you."

"What do you mean? She needed me?" Skylor was not sure that what Arlyn had said was true.

"She did, Skylor. It's what she does, as I said. Without someone to help or pray for, she feels lost."

"I see." Skylor stared across the back yard, seeing the trees and farmer's field in her line of sight. "How do we do this, Arlyn? How can we do this? I don't want harm to come to anyone."

"We'll do the best that we can to ensure that doesn't happen." Arlyn sat quietly for a while. "What do you need?"

"What do I need?" Skylor gave a harsh laugh before she was on her feet and running for her apartment.

Arlyn had jumped up as Skylor had, watching with concern as she ran. All he could was pray for her.

—

Chapter 8

Skylor wandered the town the next day, reveling in her freedom to do just that. She had never had the freedom to do so. She didn't have any money to buy anything and that stressed her. Skylor didn't see Briar watching her before he approached her.

"Skylor?" Briar's voice had her jumping. "What do you need?"

Skylor stared up at him, shrugging. She wasn't ready to ask for help. She had never worked and had never been provided with any money.

"I don't have any money, Briar. I can't buy anything." She blinked rapidly as tears threatened to engulf her.

Briar gave a muted sound and then just swept an arm around her as he nudged her into a nearby cafe and then to a seat. He pulled out a chair across from her and waved in acknowledgement to the server.

Skylor wiped at her face before a napkin was waved in her face. She took it and used it instead of her hands. She didn't see Briar take his phone out and send a message to Arlyn.

Arlyn stared at his phone before he was running for his truck and heading to find his brother. He was dismayed at the fact that Skylor was out there on her own and with no money. That was not something that he even thought about and should have. All he could do was pray for his lady. He didn't realize that Skylor was already working her way into his heart.

Skylor looked up as a chair was pulled back beside her. She frowned at Arlyn, not sure how he knew that she was there. She didn't realize that Briar had simply messaged his brother. Briar frowned at her, realizing that she not likely had a phone and he would rectify that as soon as he could before he realized that Arlyn likely had already done that.

"Skylor? You're having a good time?" Arlyn's voice was low, a frown on his face as he saw the traces of tears on her face. "Talk to me, love. Tell me what's wrong." He shook his head as Briar moved to stand and walk away.

"I'm lost, Arlyn. I have no idea how the world works. I have never had the freedom just to be out on my own. I have no friends. And I have no money and no way to make any." She looked at him, a sober look on her face. She was devastated at having to admit that. She was well aware that God was providing for her but that didn't change that fact.

"You don't, do you? We'll look after you. In fact, you can work with me. I'll teach you how to do the office work for me. That would free me up to do my research that I need to do." Arlyn heard Briar's sound of agreement. "That way, you can stay safe as well." He bit at his lip. "How does that sound?"

Skylor shrugged before her attention went to the menu that had been set in front of her. She had never seen one before and had no idea what to order.

"I can't do this, Arlyn." Her voice was barely a whisper. "I can't order. I've never seen a menu before."

Arlyn drew in a deep breath even as he heard Briar muttering to himself. He really didn't want to hear Briar's words, knowing that they would match his own.

"We'll order for you, love. Let me go over everything with you. You make the choice of what you want to eat. We will back you on any decision you make unless you are in danger. Do you understand that?"

Skylor had looked up at Arlyn as he spoke, seeing the sincerity in his face. She nodded. She could do this, she decided.

"Okay, I guess. I have never worked." Skylor blinked, a frown appearing on her face. "How do I learn?"

"We'll learn together, love. And we'll start tomorrow. I'm not in the office every day but that's okay. You can come with me if you like and learn about the birds I monitor." Arlyn grinned at her, a thought niggling at his mind that this was not likely a good idea. He was a danger to himself and likely all those around him. Arlyn just didn't know why.

The next morning found Skylor standing on the back deck, facing the door. She hadn't knocked or anything like that. She just waited for Arlyn to appear. Skylor didn't realize just how early it was. The sun had barely crept over the horizon. She sighed at last and dropped into a chair, her eyes on the yard. She listened to the birds and other critters as they awoke for the day.

<hr>

Arlyn stretched and yawned as he flipped on the coffee pot and then reached for bread to make toast. He frowned as he stared out of the large kitchen window. He rubbed at his eyes and frowned once more. Skylor really was sitting out there. He reached to make more toast and pour another cup of coffee before he loaded it all onto a tray and headed out to find her.

Skylor jumped as she heard the door before she turned towards it, her eyes huge with fright.

"Skylor? How long have you been sitting there?" Arlyn grinned at her.

Skylor shrugged. She had no idea how long that she had been out there. For a while, she knew.

Arlyn simply reached for her hand and bowed to pray for her. He peppered his prayer with all the promises that he could think of and those that God brought to his mind. He felt her hand relax in his as the prayer concluded.

"Eager to start work?" He grinned at her.

Skylor gave a small smile, her eyes on her plate. She was eager to start work but scared as well. Her dreams or nightmares had been strewn with visions of her father and his threats towards her. She didn't think that she would ever be free of him.

"I guess. I just didn't sleep very well. I don't think that he'll let me go. He'll find out where I am and drag me back to my home town." She didn't put into words that she knew that he would kill her even before that happened. Those had been his threats.

—

"That's not happening, Skylor. We'll do everything that we can to protect you. In fact, Joe is reaching out to a friend in your town. He's a detective and can work on this on the quiet. I take it that you're not sure about the police force there." Arlyn bit into a piece of his toast and chewed it as he watched her fidget with hers. "Eat, love, and then we'll head for my office. It's in what was the attached garage."

"It is? And he will?" Skylor felt hope being to spring up in her heart. "Can we really stop him?"

"We can. We might not like what happens to us while we do, but we will stop him. That's my promise and I always keep my promises." Arlyn's steady gaze reassured Skylor and warmed her heart.

Chapter 9

Late that afternoon, Arlyn turned from his front door, having opened it to Joe. He saw his aunt walking towards them as well. He sighed. Today had been an eye-opening day for him. He could only pray for his new friend, that God would heal her and then protect her. Arlyn wasn't sure that he could do that.

"Arlyn? Where's Skylor?" Joe was looking for her, sure that she would be with Arlyn.

"She's in her apartment, Joe. Today was extremely stressful for her. She's out in a world that she's never been out in before. That has exhausted her." Arlyn thought back over the day.

Skylor had stood inside the door to his office, not moving forward until he told her that she could. He had frowned at that, not sure what was happening to her. He didn't realize that she had never been allowed to move freely through rooms. Skylor had to have permission to do so.

"Skylor? It's okay. You're free to move around here." Arlyn grinned as she stared at him in shock and then astonishment. "It's okay. You need to do this. And you can do this." He drew in a deep breath.

Skylor had nodded before she cautiously began to walk through the room. She would stop every few feet to study either a photo or a bird that had been done by a taxidermist. She was astonished at the number of exhibits that Arlyn had.

Turning to Arlyn, Skylor walked to where he had seated himself at his desk and dropped into a chair in front of him. She didn't feel safe, though. She could sense the danger approaching them. She just didn't know if it was directed at her or at Arlyn.

Arlyn looked up from his paperwork, his eyes stern as he studied the lady across from him. She seemed somewhat more relaxed but not totally. He sat back, his pen dropping to the desk.

"Skylor? What can I do for you?" He grinned at her.

Skylor shrugged. She wasn't sure what to say.

"I don't know, Arlyn. I really don't." Her head turned to study the walls and shelves and cabinets. "You have a lot in here."

"I do. It's been a work in progress since I was a child." Arlyn continued to grin at her. "What do you want to know?"

Skylor shrugged before she turned to stare at the other desk. A computer sat there. Arlyn had turned it on and then walked away, not realizing that she had no idea what to do.

"The computer, Arlyn? I don't know how to work it. I've never seen one before." A sob rose as she spoke. "I was never allowed one. And the phone? I've never seen one of those before. Dad had one but it was always locked in his bedroom. I wasn't allowed to see it or even use it."

Arlyn stared at her in horror. He understood to some extent what she had been saying. He just didn't realize it had been that bad. He was on his feet, his hand reaching for hers, and then drawing her to a seat behind the desk.

"Here, I'll teach you." Arlyn knelt beside her, an arm resting on the back of her chair. He didn't understand that this made her uncomfortable at first before she felt peace from God flowing through her as she turned her head to watch him, taken aback at how close he was to her.

Arlyn began the process of teaching Skylor how to use the computer, patient as she fumbled her way through the beginning of the process.

"I have a computer that I'll set up downstairs for you, Skylor." He shook his head at her protest. "It's okay. I don't use it. You can work away on it as you want and surf the internet as well."

Skylor's brow was lowered as she frowned at him. She had not expected that. In fact, she expected nothing. That had been Skylor's life for as long as she could remember.

"You would do that?"

"I would. You need to take back your life and this is part of how you do it. There is no pressure or timeline to do that, Skylor. We'll work with you in everything. If you're not comfortable talking to me, Briar, or Cayce, talk to Aunt Anna. She'll want that." Arlyn was on his feet, his hand reaching for Skylor's one more. "For now, we'll pack it in for the day and then pick it up tomorrow." He groaned. "Tomorrow I have to be out in the field. You'll come, won't you?"

Skylor rose, her hand tight in Arlyn's. She wasn't used to contact that was so caring and tender. She had no idea how to react. She simply prayed for understanding and then protection for Arlyn.

Coming back to the present, Arlyn stared at Joe. He nodded. Joe needed to speak with Skylor.

"Let me find her." Arlyn was away to tap at the outside door to Skylor's apartment. He simply grinned at her as he reached to pull her through the door and then locked it behind her. "Joe's here and needs to speak with you."

Skylor tugged her hand from his. She stood her ground, not moving forward, a frown on her face.

"And you couldn't just ask me?" Skylor was afraid suddenly, her body cowering back from Arlyn. She was sure that he would strike out at her.

"I'm sorry. I should have. I need to learn to do that. Skylor, Joe is looking for you. Would you come upstairs to speak with him?" Arlyn stood watching, seeing the change in her and then sorrowing because he had caused it.

Skylor walked away from him, heading to his home to find Joe waiting for her. She frowned at the look on his face before she turned away from him and just began to prepare a meal. She felt Anna hug her and then reach to help with the meal.

Joe shared a look with Arlyn before he shrugged. He heard Briar and Cayce behind him and sighed. This is not how this was to go. He really did have to speak with Skylor. He had information about her family that he needed to discuss with her.

Arlyn drew Joe away from the four in the kitchen and to his home office. He paced even as he watched Joe.

"Joe? What can you tell me?" Arlyn finally planted himself in front of Joe.

Joe shook his head. He did need to speak with Arlyn as well but he had wanted to speak with Skylor first.

"Not a lot, Arlyn. Unfortunately, not a lot. There was no evidence on that photo. We could see where your truck was rammed from behind and sending you off the road. Other than that, we don't know why or who. I don't see you having any enemies that you are aware of."

"No, I don't see that I do. But with my work? It's possible that someone is out to take over what I do or to discredit me. My reputation could be damaged to the point where I could no longer fulfill what I want to with my work." Arlyn had always been afraid of that.

"I know that. We're trying to find out what. We've gone to the people on the street to see if there is anything there." Joe was frustrated at that.

"I know that you are." Arlyn looked past Joe and then moved to reach for Skylor's hand. He sensed her hesitation at physical contact with him before she reached for his hand. He drew her into the office. "Is supper ready?"

"Just about." She frowned at Joe, seeing his easy grin at her.

"Do you have a few moments, Skylor? I do need to speak with you."

Skylor scowled at him before she tugged her hand free and walked away. Arlyn had a small smile on his face as he watched her. Joe just stared at her in disbelief as she walked away from him once more.

"She'll keep doing that, Joe. She's finding freedom and is struggling to adjust. It's difficult for her. I learned today that she didn't even know what a phone was like. The only one in her home was locked in her father's bedroom. And she has no idea of what a computer is or does."

Joe's head had swung around as Arlyn spoke. His eyes slid closed. This was even worse than he thought.

"It was that bad?" Joe walked away to find Skylor, finding her ignoring him for the moment.

Chapter 10

Wiping his hands on his paper napkin, Arlyn watched Skylor closely. He could tell that she was highly stressed and trying had to hide it. He reached for her hand, his warm on hers and that stilled her uneasy movements.

"Can we pray before Joe speaks with Skylor? She needs that." Briar spoke up, watching his brother's care for the lady beside him.

"We can do that." Cayce bowed his head, doing just that. He heard the prayers of the others before his head was raised and he was watching Skylor closely.

"Skylor?" Joe waited until she looked at him. "Do you want to speak in private or do you want them here?" He was giving her a choice that normally would not have been hers to make.

"I can make the choice?" Skylor stared at him. "I can say what I want?"

"You can, Skylor. And we back your decisions unless you are in danger. Then, we step in but explain exactly why. You deserve that." Joe smiled at her, patiently waiting on her decision.

"I guess here, then. They need to know what is going on. I don't want them hurt." Skylor found Arlyn's hand tightening on hers as he agreed silently with her decision.

"Okay, then. I have spoken with my friend in your town." His hand went up as Joe stopped her

———

words. "He is not investigating this at the detachment. He is working on it at home. We also have a friend who is a private investigator that we can reach out to if we feel we need to." Joe reached for the folder that he had dropped under his chair. "I can share some of what we have found, Skylor. And I think it will help you to understand what you are going through."

Joe handed over a photo to Skylor. She stared at it, not recognizing it.

"Who is this?" Skylor looked up at Joe. "Who is it?"

"It's the lady who we believe is your mother . What were you told about her?"

Skylor shrugged, not sure what she had been told.

"I don't remember being told anything. If I asked when I was young, the question was ignored. How did you find her?"

"It wasn't hard, Skylor. She's been looking for you all your life. She was kicked out of the house when you were only three months old and not allowed any contact with you. In fact, your father drove her from town and to another town. She was never able to return to your town." Joe watched as Skylor's face crumpled and she wept. Joe had been told this. He just didn't think that it was the truth.

Skylor looked up at last, sorrow in her heart. Her mother, who she had begged God to bring into her life, had been looking for her all along. She just didn't understand who God had allowed that.

———

"What else, Joe? What else do I need to know?" They all could hear the anger in her voice and knew that it was justified.

"Your father has disappeared. We don't know where he is but the thinking is that he is searching for you. How did you ever get away?" Joe was puzzled at that.

Skylor shrugged. She had wondered the same thing as well.

"I don't know. For once, my bedroom door was not locked when my father was out of the house. I walked to the back door and it was unlocked. It never was. I returned to my bedroom, taking one of his backpacks, and packed some stuff. Did I do right?"

Arlyn was on his feet, heading for her apartment and then returning with the backpack. He had a horrible thought that this was planned by her father and that there was a tracking device in the pack. He handed it to Joe who nodded before he began to search it.

"You're wondering what we're doing, aren't you?" Joe waited for Skylor to nod. "It is odd that the doors were unlocked. We searched your backpack to ensure that there was nothing to show that you were being tracked." He nodded at Arlyn, who simply reached for Skylor's shoes where they sat near the back door and searched them as well. He drew in a breath of relief. "It doesn't look as if he is able to track you. And that is good." He smiled at her.

"He could do that?" Skylor was shocked at that. She wasn't aware that people could be tracked without someone following them. "Then, how did the doors get unlocked?"

"I don't know, Skylor. Nor does my friend. We are working on that but so far, no one is saying anything. You had a friend there who stepped in to help you." Joe looked into the folder once more. "We have confirmed that you are due an inheritance when you turn thirty. It was to go to your father if you died or were declared mentally incompetent at that point. That is likely why he kept you locked in your home."

"I don't want it. I don't want it. If that's why I was caged all my life, I don't want it." Skylor began to sob, finding Arlyn just reaching to wrap her into a hug. Her heartbroken cries disturbed them all. They could not comprehend what her life had been like or the depravity of someone who would do that.

"Joe? I have a question." Cayce was careful to keep his voice low and even. "How do we know that the man is her father?"

Joe stared at him and nodded.

"That's one lead that we're looking into. It will take time and time is something that Skylor may not have. We'll do a DNA match on both the father and the woman claiming to be her mother. And then we go from there." Joe turned as Anna made a sound. "Anna?"

"Joe, I don't want to suggest how you do your work. I know you too well to do that. What if Skylor was not their child?" Anna kept her eyes on Skylor, finding that lady had turned to stare at her, an unreadable look in her eyes.

"We had that thought as well. Skylor? We need to do a buccal swab to obtain your DNA/"

"What is that?"

"We use a swab to take a sample from inside your cheek. And then we send it to a lab to have them work on it as we say and retrieve whatever it is that they need to in order to provide a panel of your DNA to compare to other DNA."

"That sounds too complicated." Skylor leaned back on Arlyn, not realizing that she had done so and that his arms were still holding her.

"It is but it's done a lot." Joe excused himself at that point, needing to be at a meeting.

Skylor watched him walk away, a frown on her face. She needed to think and pray through what Joe had said and also to determine how she could find out the truth.

Chapter 11

Arlyn shifted the backpack that he was wearing as he paused along a local trail. He watched as Skylor spun in a circle, a happy look on her face. He didn't think that he had seen that emotion on her face in the few days that he had known her.

"Happy, Skylor?" He grinned at her.

"I am. I have never had this freedom before. Now what do we do?" Skylor was watching Arlyn carefully and was following the cues that he was giving off.

"We look for a certain bird that is in this area." His phone was out as he showed her a picture. "I don't see it very often and that concerns me."

"What is that bird?"

"A red-headed woodpecker. I haven't seen one in weeks." He looked around. "This is where I usually see them."

"So, what do we do?" Skylor was watching Arlyn closely, ready to take a cue on how she was to act from him.

"We wait and we watch. If we don't see one today, then we come back and more somewhere else close to here." Arlyn dropped his pack to the ground, looking around. "I think we're good here for now, Skylor."

Two hours later, Arlyn rose, shouldered his pack, and reached for Skylor's hand. He had been doing that a lot that day and she had just accepted it. She had no idea why he would want to hold her hand.

"Are we done now?" Skylor's voice was low, disappointment evident in it.

"We are. We'll come back in a day or so, love." Arlyn led them back down the path towards his truck. His steps slowed, however, as he neared the parking lot, hearing angry voices. "Wait here, Skylor." He tried to shake her hand loose but hers tightened on his. She was just not going to let him leave her alone. "Skylor? I need you to wait here."

Skylor was shaking her head. There was no way that she was staying anywhere on her own. She just pointed towards the parking lot and started walking forward.

Arlyn sighed and then walked rapidly after her, her hand tugging him with her. They paused at the edge of the path, watching the men milling around. There were three of them and Arlyn decided that they didn't have their good in mind. He looked around for shelter and tugged Skylor with him that time. She frowned at him before her attention went back to the men.

"Skylor? Do you know those men?"

Skylor shook her head. She had no idea who they were. She had had no contact with anyone other than her father. How would she know them?

Arlyn sighed. Those men were not there for their good, he didn't think. They couldn't reach his rental truck. He looked around, searching for a way to escape and not seeing one. He heard the sharp intake of Skylor's breath and looked around to see a weapon held on them. Arlyn's heart dropped. This was what he had been trying to avoid. He could only pray that God protected them and released them from these men.

They waited for what seemed like hours, waiting for what Skylor and Arlyn were never sure of. The men paced away from them and then back. Arlyn was on the alert, ready to shove Skylor ahead of him and run. He knew the area very well, having studied it and spent hours there. The opportunity finally came as the men walked back to the pavement. Arlyn shoved Skylor ahead of him to a game path and then followed her, their steps as quiet as they could make them. Arlyn moved around Skylor to take the lead, his hand reaching for hers.

Skylor kept pace with him, not sure why they were running along such a narrow path, doing the branches and shrubs that lashed at her. She trusted Arlyn in a way that she never thought that she would trust anyone.

Arlyn slowed his steps, coming to a halt and wrapping Skylor into a hug. He searched the area, not seeing anyone around who would cause them harm. He pulled her with him towards the sidewalk that they could see.

Skylor had no idea where they were or where Arlyn was heading. All she knew was that she was deeply afraid and didn't know whether Arlyn would even be able to protect her. She finally pulled him to a stop.

—

"Arlyn? Where are we? And just who were those men?" Skylor looked behind her, not believing that they had been able to escape. She had heard the yells of rage that had followed their disappearance.

"I have no idea, Skylor. For now, we are safe. We're only about ten blocks from my home." He almost ran towards his home, Skylor keeping pace with him. He locked them inside his home, not letting Skylor head to her apartment. "We need to talk to Joe, if he's around."

Skylor shrugged and then headed outside and to her apartment. She refused to let him lock her in with him. Arlyn followed her and then stood watching as she closed him out. He didn't want that but knew that she needed that.

Skylor sank to the floor with her back to the door. She had locked herself in, the only way that she felt safe, even as she hated to have a locked door. Skylor knew better than to leave it unlocked.

Arlyn walked slowly back into his house, disturbed at what had happened and how it had affected Skylor. He had prayed for safety that day but God had allowed this. He had to accept that. He just didn't know how to protect her and help her to come to terms with what had happened in her life.

Joe turned from the crime scene that he had been working. He reached for his phone to check his messages and frowned at the one from Arlyn. He headed for that parking lot, not seeing the men but knowing that Arlyn would not have reacted as he had if he had not been afraid. Joe stared at Arlyn's rental truck before he was searching it. Satisfied that it was fine, he turned back to his car, pausing at he saw Briar walking towards him.

"Briar?" Joe frowned at him. "What are you doing here?"

"Retrieving Arlyn's truck. He called me." Briar looked around, feeling unsafe and watched. "Someone is out there."

"There is. Head off, Briar. I've checked it out and it seems fine." Joe walked back to his car, intent on following Briar. He feared for his friends, knowing that this was far from over for them.

Arlyn turned as Briar handed over his keys and then stared at Joe. Of course, Joe would be there.

"Joe?"

"I searched your truck, Arlyn. It was fine. Now, where is Skylor? You both need to talk to me." Joe was stern, part of that to hide his fear for his friends.

Chapter 12

Skylor refused to leave her apartment despite the pleading that Arlyn was giving. She refused to unlock her door. She had been badly frightened that day and didn't want to be around anyone. She just sank back into herself as she always had done.

Arlyn turned to Joe and shrugged. He had no idea how to reach out to her at this point. He had to let her have the evening and then work with her once more. Anna hugged him and then headed for Skylor. Skylor was not surprised to see her even though she wanted to be on her own. Anna simply moved quietly in on her and hugged her, praying for the young lady who had become an important part of their lives.

Skylor wrapped her arms around her waist, so afraid that she couldn't move. Anna kept glancing at her as she prepared tea and toast for them before she piled it all on a tray and carried it into the living room. Anna then returned to wrap an arm around Skylor and guided her to a seat on the couch. She then bowed her head and began to pray audibly for her young friend.

"Skylor? What happened? Something did to cause you to freeze like this. Were you threatened?" Anna waited patiently for Skylor to speak. She would wait for as long as it took.

"I don't know, Anna. I was out with Arlyn today in the woods. We walked back to where he had parked and three men took us hostage. They held a gun towards me to make Arlyn do what they wanted to." Skylor was sober as she said that. "They walked away from us and Arlyn made us walk along a narrow path. I think he called it a game path." She was almost in tears, her emotions were that raw, and she was so afraid.

"You need to tell this to Joe, you know. He's upstairs." Anna hugged Skylor before she was on her feet and heading to find Joe.

Joe followed Anna quietly, his eyes watching Skylor. She was very near to the edge of breaking, he could tell, and that distressed him. He sat, his eyes on her, praying for a touch of the garment for her and for full healing.

Skylor looked up at Joe, not sure what to say or how he would want her to respond. She sighed and then simply stated what had happened and that she had no idea who the men were. She had never seen them before.

Joe nodded, his notes made before he tucked away his notebook. He didn't know how to help her, he knew. He would have to find someone who could help her.

The next morning, Arlyn walked out of his house and into his office. He looked around, not sure what he was planning on doing that day. That was not him. He turned as he heard hesitant footsteps coming through the outside door and faced Skylor. She refused to look at him, instead heading for the smaller desk and the work that was waiting there. She just didn't know what to do with the paperwork.

Arlyn moved to kneel beside her, an arm around her. He prayed for her, not sure how to approach her.

He could see the dark circles under her eyes and sighed. She not likely had slept much and that worried him. He hadn't slept either, spending the night in prayer.

"Skylor? Talk to me. Tell me what you are feeling." Arlyn was almost begging her to do that.

Skylor shrugged. She had buried the events from the day before deep inside her. She didn't want to bring it back up again. As far as Skylor was concerned, going back over it would solve nothing.

"Arlyn? What is going on? Who is after you? And why?" Skylor stared at him, a sober look on her face. She was not scared. She had been through too much in her life to be scared by the men.

"Skylor? Are you okay?" Arlyn tilted his head to study her closer. "Talk to me. Tell me what is going on."

Skylor shrugged once more. She didn't know how to react or what to say.

"Arlyn? You need to work. I'll be fine. Go on." She shooed him away towards his own desk.

Arlyn sat, his eyes on Skylor. He watched as she sorted through what was on her desk and then woke the computer up. She was sitting staring at it and he could tell that she had very little idea of what to do. He sighed before he picked up the work that he needed to get through.

Skylor was on her feet two hours later. She had tried her best to work but she had no idea what to do or what exactly was expected of her. She walked from the office and down to her apartment. Grabbing a bottle of water, Skylor headed for her bedroom and threw herself on her bed. Tears clogged her throat but she refused to let them free. She slept at last, not hearing the tapping at her door.

Anna turned from the door before she headed for Arlyn. She looked down at the letter that she was holding, a threat against herself. She stood for a moment, watching Arlyn before she walked into the office and brought his attention to himself.

"Aunt Anna?" Arlyn was on his feet, frowning at Anna. "What's that?"

"This? This letter? It's a threat against me, Arlyn. Who is doing this?" Anna shook the letter at him.

"What?" Arlyn reached for the letter, opening it and reading it. "This is brutal, Aunt Anna. We need to find Joe."

"I've already called him. He'll be here when he can." Anna looked around. "Where's Skylor?"

Arlyn blinked at his aunt in surprise and then looked over to where he had last seen Skylor.

"She's not here ?" Arlyn was out of the office and knocking at Skylor's door. He frowned. She was not answering. He then ran for his home office and drew up the video feed, seeing her entering her apartment and not leaving. He drew in a deep breath of relief but that didn't excuse him for not seeing her leave. That should not have happened but he knew that

Skylor would not have disturbed him to tell him that she was leaving.

"I'm sorry, Aunt Anna. I didn't know that she left. I need to do better." Sadness covered his face. "She would not say anything in case that she disturbed me. It's who she is."

"It is, Arlyn. It is. We need to work with her and that will take time. She's what, 28 or 29?" At his nod, Anna looked around, not sure what to say. "God has been with her all those years, Arlyn. She still has a lot of trauma that she will need to deal with and that will take months if not years."

"She will." Arlyn walked away as he heard a tap at the front door and opened it to find Joe standing there. "Joe?"

"Where's your aunt?" Joe was almost harsh with his words. "She called me and then said that she was heading here."

"She's here." Arlyn watched at Joe walked towards Anna. He reached for his phone and called Skylor, not expecting her to answer.

"Hello?" Skylor was still groggy from being awoken.

"Skylor? Are you awake?" Laughter sprinkled through his voice.

"I am now. What do you want?" Skylor sat up, brushing her hair from her face.

"Joe is here. He needs to speak with you. I'm coming to your door." Arlyn walked towards her apartment door. "And I'm sorry that I ignored you."

Chapter 13

Skylor refused to speak to Joe, just standing away from him and watching him. Joe didn't know what to say to get her to open up to him. He had never had a victim such as this.

"Skylor? Are you okay?" Joe continued to press her to speak.

Skylor simply stared at him and then walked away from him, heading for the outdoors. She slumped into a chair, her eyes closing. She was praying but didn't think that her prayers were going anywhere. A worn Bible had been the book that she had chosen most often to read and had read it many times over the years, memorizing verses while she was desperate to understand fully what it all meant.

Joe stared dumbfounded after Skylor. He really didn't know what to say. He watched as Anna walked after Skylor, praying that Anna would be able to reach through to her. He just didn't know if someone would be able.

"Joe? She'll do that. She'll walk away from us, just trying to keep herself sane and safe." Arlyn shook his head at his friend. "What do you think about that letter?"

"The letter? It is a direct threat at your aunt. They are going after your family because they can't get to you. You've escaped them twice and they will not accept a third escape on your part. This letter directly references you, not Skylor. Skylor's case is separate from this, that we know."

"And how is that case going?" Arlyn was frustrated, to say the least. "How do I keep her safe?"

"You can't, Arlyn. Even if she was your wife, you can't keep her safe. We're still working on it but have to set it aside for now. You know how this works. We need to wait for investigations to work through the evidence."

"And you're saying that you don't have much information, aren't you?" Arlyn was frustrated once more. He walked away from Joe to stand at the kitchen window and watch Skylor and his aunt. There had to be some way to figure out what was going on and now. He just didn't see the way to do that. He walked then to his office, seating himself and then immersing himself in his work. He didn't hear the activity that increased outside of his house or Skylor's cry for help.

Skylor lay motionless on the backyard, not hearing the sounds of the men running away. She had been beaten and left out in the open. The skies had been heavy with rain all day. The rain began, heavy at times, soaking her and then moving on to another area. She didn't rouse at all.

Arlyn rose at last, stretching and then reaching to turn off the lights and head into the house. He frowned at the clock before he headed to change to more casual clothes. He always wore more dress clothes in the office.

Reaching for his phone, Arlyn sent a text to Skylor, frowning when she didn't respond. He didn't like that.   He headed for her apartment door, hammering at it and not receiving a response.   He turned as he heard his name called. Briar and Cayce were walking towards him, bags of food in their hands.

"Arlyn? You're finished for the day?" Cayce walked past him, frowning. "Where's Skylor?"

"In her apartment, I think. It has not been a good day. I can't get her to answer." Arlyn reached for his keys, reluctant to enter her home but knowing that he needed to, given the circumstances.

"Do that. We'll put out our meal. Hopefully, she'll join us." Briar hesitated and then waited for his brother. He was not prepared for Arlyn to shoot back out of the door, panic on his face. "Arlyn?"

"She's not there. Where is she?"

Briar gave a yell for Cayce before he began to search. Cayce headed for the backyard and then began to search.   Cayce was not prepared to trip over something in the dusk, hitting his hands and knees. He spun on his knees, a hand reaching out to touch what he had tripped over. A shout rose to his lips as he felt the body and realized that it was Skylor.

Arlyn raced for his brother, shock on his face as he saw that Cayce was working on Skylor. He was on his knees, reaching to help, dismayed as felt the soaked condition of her clothes.

"Cayce?"

"I tripped over her, Arlyn. I didn't see her in the dark. Briar?" His shout reached to Briar.

"I've called it in. How long?" Briar bent over, a hand on Arlyn's shoulder, feeling the tenseness of his brother's muscles.

"Long enough to become totally soaked." Cayce looked up for a moment before Briar nodded, running to the house and returning with a thick blanket. Cayce took it with thanks, tucking it around Skylor. "Skylor? When did you last see her?"

"This morning. She left the office after a couple of hours. Aunt Anna talked with her. Aunt Anna received a threatening letter and called Joe. He spoke with Skylor again but that didn't go over very well. She is just not opening up as he wants her to." Arlyn was more than disturbed at this.

"And she won't. She doesn't know any other way of life other than to stay silent and stay hidden. It will take a long time to get her over that, if she ever can." Briar headed for the front yard as he heard the sirens, beckoning them to the backyard.

Joe watched the activity from the sidelines. He had caught the call just as he was leaving the office and headed for his friends. He had expected something to happen but he had not expected it to be so soon. He turned to Cayce as that man stood beside him.

"Can you access his security feed?"

"I can. Come on. Arlyn's not leaving her, and Briar's not leaving Arlyn." Cayce walked into his brother's home and to his office, pulling up the video feed. He stared at it as Joe bent forward from beside him to watch, a hand resting on the back of the leather office chair.

—

"You can't see much, can you? And the rain started about the time the men attacked her. I don't get why." Cayce sat back, not sure what he was seeing or the reason for it.

"I'll need a copy of that, Cayce." Joe was frustrated that he couldn't make out the features of the men and that Skylor was just left in the rain without any thought of how it would affect her.

—

Chapter 14

Arlyn paced the waiting room at the local hospital. Skylor had not responded, not while she was being worked on or on the drive to the hospital. He had simply jumped up into the rig without saying anything, drawing glances at himself.

Joe had appeared, stopping by the clerk. He simply asked that Arlyn and Anna be added to Skylor's chat, stating that she had no family in the area. He was then through the doors and looking for the physician who was treating her.

"Doc? What's the word?" Joe would not keep him long, looking around at the busy and overcrowded emergency rooms.

"She's soaked through, Joe. And she has been beaten. Who is she?" The physician looked around at Joe, seeing his hesitation in answering the questions. "Joe?"

Joe nodded, the scent associated with a hospital filling his nostrils. This was not where he wanted to be and felt that he had been here way too many times.

"She's new to town. She's a friend of Arlyn's."

"Arlyn's? I didn't think that he was dating." The physician reached to switch off the light box that held X-ray images.

"He's not, not that we know of. Skylor and he are mixed up in something. She's not from our town. Just so you know? She just escaped captivity in her own home. Her father held her captive all of her life and from what she has said, abused her physically and emotionally."

The physician paused, his eyes on the room door to where Skylor lay.

"That explains it. I can see old fractures, some of which didn't heal the best. Find him and don't ever let him near her again." He paused before he looked towards the waiting room. "Arlyn's out there?"

"He is. So are Briar, Cayce, and Anna." Joe walked away at last, not satisfied that they were able to rightly determine how to protect her. He had no idea why she had been out there on her own. And Arlyn was not a lot of help.

Arlyn was on his feet as the nurse approached him, Anna beside him. They followed her, hesitating in the doorway to the room before Arlyn was across the room and beside the stretcher. A hand was rested against her hair as Arlyn almost wept at how she looked. Anna wrapped an arm around her nephew. This was one time that she could not heal his breaking heart.

Cayce turned his head as he heard footsteps and then was on his feet. Briar frowned at him before he too was on his feet, hugging his mother. Their parents had appeared, just at the right time, Cayce decided.

Ardan and Bessie hugged their two sons before they looked around. They didn't see Arlyn and that worried them. Joe had reached out to them, simply stating that they were needed at the hospital and wondered just where they were. They had just arrived home and started sorting out what they had to do. They had dropped everything and simply headed for their sons, praying for them as they did so.

"Where's Arlyn?" Bessie sat between the two younger men. "Has he been hurt?"

"Not at all, Mom. He and Aunt Anna are back with Skylor." Briar shared a look with Cayce. "We need to talk with you and let you know exactly what has happened."

Bessie had stared at her sons in horror as she heard about Skylor. She shared a look with Ardan, determined that she would find that lady and help her to heal.

"He's back with her?" Ardan paced away from his family, a disturbed look on his face.

Cayce was on his feet, a hand to his father's back to direct him outside. It was dark, but that didn't matter to either the father or the son.

"Cayce? What's going on with Arlyn?" Ardan was confused for a moment.

"Someone is after him, Dad. We don't know why or who. Joe has been investigating but he's not getting too far. There's just a sense of danger around him."

Ardan nodded. He had often felt worried about Arlyn's work. He knew that there was a black market out there for endangered birds and body parts. He had prayed that it would not come near him.

Cayce finally turned his father back into the waiting room, finding Arlyn walking towards him.

Anna had found Bessie and sat beside her. Arlyn nodded at Cayce who sighed to himself. This could not be good news about Skylor.

"Dad?" Arlyn reached to hug his father before he stepped back. "When did you and Mom get home?"

"A couple of hours ago. What is the situation, son?"

"Skylor is still unconscious. She was beaten, Dad, and then left in the rain. I didn't hear a thing. I was working and didn't know that she had left the office." Arlyn was not clear with his words, causing Ardan to frown at him and then at his other sons.

"Skylor is working in his office, Dad." Briar studied his oldest brother. "At least, she's trying to. She has had no contact with anyone other than her father for her whole life."

"She hasn't? And why would that be?" Ardan paced away from his sons before he turned to study the three of them. His eyes lingered on Arlyn, seeing the devastation and worry that Arlyn was trying hard to hide. "Son? What are your thoughts?" Ardan's hand landed on Arlyn's shoulders. "What do you want to do?"

Arlyn shrugged. He had been pondering that very question. He had no idea what to say or what to do. He turned and walked away from his father and headed for Skylor.

Standing beside the stretcher, Arlyn watched the lady who was working her way into his heart. He was desperately worried about her but didn't know how to go ahead with whatever it was that he needed to do. His hand rested on Skylor's cheek, praying for her, begging God to heal her. She needed those prayers and that healing.

He finally walked away, heading back for the waiting room. He didn't want to, knowing that his family would be waiting for him. He searched for them, seeing only his mother waiting for him. He sank down beside her, returning her hug before he buried his head in his hands.

"How is she?" Bessie was worried about her son. She frowned as he didn't respond right away.

Arlyn shrugged. He had no words to describe how she was.

"I don't know, Mom. I really don't know. It's not the first beating that she's taken over her life. I just pray that it's the last."

Bessie stared at him. She had no idea what he was talking about.

"Arlyn? What do you mean? Where are her parents? They should be here."

"No, they shouldn't. I have no idea where her mother is or even if she's still alive. Skylor has no memory of her. And as to her father? I pray that he stays away. He was physically and emotionally abusive to her all of her life." Arlyn turned his face towards his mother, determination mixed with anger on it. "He kept her locked away until just a couple of weeks ago. She was never allowed out anywhere. She has no knowledge of how the world works."

—

Bessie drew in a deep breath. She had not been aware that was what Skylor had faced. She prayed for the young lady who seemed to be claiming her son's attention. She wanted to be her mother and would certainly reach out to her. For now? All Bessie could do was wrap an arm around her hurting son and pray for him.

Chapter 15

Skylor roused at last, not sure where she was and only that she felt safe. She cracked her eyes open just a hair and looked around, frowning. She had no idea where she was. Shifting to her side, Skylor tugged the blankets up and around her neck, snuggling down into the warmth. She winced as she hit the soreness on her side before her face became the blank slate that it always was.

Sleeping once more, Skylor didn't hear the sounds of the medical staff that moved around her overnight or Arlyn touching her hair in the early morning. She just didn't rouse. That worried Arlyn until the staff explained that this was normal and that she would rouse at some point.

Arlyn paced away at last. He had meetings that he needed to be at but he really didn't want to leave. He would be back as soon as he was able to, provided that Skylor was still there. He had spoken with his aunt and his parents about where she should go. He realized that he could not make that decision for her but had to let her make her own decision as to where she wanted to be. All Arlyn could do was to pray for her and that he had been doing constantly.

Anna stood for a moment, an arm around Bessie as she hesitated in the doorway. Bessie wasn't sure if she should even be there even though Arlyn had asked her to. He just wanted a mother for Skylor and his mother was available.

—

"It's okay, Bessie. He's talked about you to her. I have heard him." Anna walked forward, a hand resting on Skylor's hair for a moment. She prayed for her young friend and her nephew, knowing that Arlyn was not prepared to walk away from Skylor.

Bessie approached Skylor, her eyes on the younger lady. She didn't understand what was happening. Not that it would have made any difference. She was worried about this young lady just because her family was.

Skylor heard the footsteps around her bed and the low conversation that the two ladies carried on. She didn't want to wake up. Not at all but she knew that she had to. She drew in a deep breath before her eyes opened. Skylor frowned at the lady standing in her line of vision.

"Skylor? Are you awake?" Anna moved into her line of sight.

"Where am I?" Skylor coughed, her throat raw from the soaking that she had undergone.

"In the hospital, Skylor. I'm told that you can leave now. Do you want to go back to your own apartment or come with me or Bessie? Bessie is Arlyn's mother and is willing to take you in."

"I want to go home. Only home is not where I should be." Skylor yawned, her thoughts muddled.

"We'll take you to your apartment then. Arlyn is at some meetings but he'll be home by the time that we get you there." Anna watched Skylor closely.

Skylor just refused to respond. She was on her feet, trying to find her clothes and then disappearing to dress. Anna and Bessie exchanged glances. This was not how they had expected Skylor to react.

Once more with the ladies, Skylor didn't speak. She didn't respond to Anna's question, simply moving away from the ladies. They followed her, not sure what they were heading. Anna's hand on Skylor's arm stopped her forward walk.

"Wait for us, Skylor. We'll get you to where you need to be but you do need to stop walking away from us." Anna's voice was gentle as she spoke. "Let's get you to your home."

"No, I can't go there." Terror flooded through Skylor. "I can't go there. My father will kill me. He said that he would."

Neither lady was able to get Skylor to respond. Anna tucked her into her car, turning as she heard Ardan speaking to her.

"Anna? Bessie?" Ardan ducked his head to stare at Skylor through the car window. "Has she spoken?"

"Other than to say that she wanted to go home?" Bessie turned to Anna. "What did she mean, that her father would kill her?"

"He would do that. She's mentioned that he had threatened her if she ever got away. We don't understand why. Joe's working on that." Anna sighed, her eyes on the horizon. "We need to figure this out. I'm not sure that we can before either Arlyn or Skylor are injured."

—

Ardan nodded. It was about what he had expected from his conversation with his sons. Arlyn had not said much but Ardan knew that his son was highly troubled. And Skylor had to be the reason for those troubled thoughts.

"Where are you heading with Skylor?" Ardan was willing to do what he could for the young lady.

"To her apartment. She'll be close to Arlyn there but also have the privacy that she needs. She's not communicating much with us. That makes it so difficult. Briar and Cayce are trying to get her to open up. She's not."

Walking through Skylor's apartment a short while later, Anna frowned. Something seemed off but she could not determine just what. She would reach out to Joe in a bit if he hadn't shown up and see what his thoughts were. Anna was deeply troubled for her young friend, knowing just how deep the fear was that Skylor had to be experiencing.

Arlyn tapped at the door and then peeked around it as he stepped through into the apartment. His mother simply hugged him before his aunt approached him.

"Aunt Anna? Skylor's here?" Arlyn was hopeful that she was, but he wasn't sure.

"She is, Arlyn. She's getting cleaned up but she's not doing well. She should not have come home yet." Anna was distraught at that. Skylor was refusing any help from them and just walking away. "She's hurting, Arlyn, and has shut down."

Arlyn nodded. It was about what he had expected to hear. He sighed. All he could do was pray for his lady, begging God to protect her. He looked up at that point, seeing Skylor standing in the shadows of the hall, her eyes on him. She was not approaching him nor speaking. He walked towards her, seeing her shaking from fear. He stopped, his hands reached out, palm up, and just waited for Skylor to respond.

It took a lot of time, Arlyn thought, before Skylor tentatively reached to lay hers in his. His fingers closed gently around hers and then his head bowed as he prayed once more for her. Skylor's eyes did not move. She simply stared at him, no expression on her face.

Tugging her gently to move forward, Arlyn coaxed Skylor to the couch where he gently shoved her down. He sat on the coffee table, watching her closely. She refused to look up at him again, instead keeping her eyes directed towards the floor. She was just too scared to do anything else.

Chapter 16

Skylor could not stop her shaking. She was just so deeply afraid. She had been sure that she heard her father in her hospital room the night before and that frightened her, not just for herself but for the people who were now around her. She just didn't know what to say or whether to say anything. Skylor was certain that she was being judged and found wanting.

Anna's arm came around Skylor, causing her to jump. Despite that, she did not look up. She could hear the quiet conversation around her and Anna's quiet prayer for her. She didn't know what to say or think. This had not been what her life had been like. Not at all.

Arlyn watched her closely, seeing how shuttered she had become. She had started to open up to him and to his family and he missed that. He rose at last and headed for the outdoors. Briar, Cayce, and Joe were walking towards him.

"Arlyn?" Briar studied his brother before he turned to face the house. "Where's Skylor?"

"In her living room. Mom, Dad, and Aunt Anna are with her. She's shut down, guys. Totally shut down. It's worse than when I first met her. And I don't know what to do to reach through to her." Arlyn drew in a deep, shuddering breath. Skylor had become more important to him than his own family. All he could do was to beg God for a touch of the garment for her and for healing and protection.

"It's to be expected, Arlyn." Joe had seen this somewhat before but not to the degree that Skylor was at. "Has she spoken at all?"

Arlyn shook his head. She was not speaking and no matter what they said to her, she just wasn't responding in any way, shape or form.

"She's just sitting on the couch, staring at the floor." Arlyn frowned as he turned to his brothers. There had never been silence between the three brothers. If anything, at times their parents had to separate them. He just didn't know how to help her. "We need to find her someone to speak with."

"And we will." Joe had reached out to a friend, asking if he knew of anyone. The friend had assured him that he did and that he would reach out to that lady. "I have a friend reaching out to someone who may be able to help. He's to get back to me in a couple of days. For now, we need to keep both of you safe. Skylor we need to protect against anyone who comes at her to take her back to her father's home or means to harm or kill her." Joe had learned to be frank with others and he knew the triplets would accept his words. "And you, Arlyn? Someone is after you because of your work. That's what I'm hearing on the streets."

Arlyn nodded, having come to both those conclusions.

"How do we do this then? We don't have enough information to do anything really." Arlyn bit at his lip, his eyes on Cayce. "Do we have a photo of her father and any friends of his? That way, we know who we're looking for."

"That's fair enough." Joe pointed towards the apartment. "I'll leave some inside for you. For now, Arlyn, what can we do for you?"

Arlyn shrugged. He had no idea what to ask for. He knew that his family and friends were praying for him. He sighed.

"I have no idea, Joe, seeing as I have never been in this situation before." Arlyn watched his father as he approached the four younger men. "Dad?"

"Arlyn, I have a question for you. Is Skylor talking to anyone?"

"No, she's not, Dad." Arlyn watched his father closely before his eyes slid closed. "Julia."

Ardan was nodding. Julia was the wife of one of his sons' friends.

"Julia. She was raised by an abusive mother and stepfather. And then there's Rachel. She was raised by an abusive foster father. Either one of those ladies would be good to speak with Skylor. I can reach out, if you like."

"Thanks, Dad. That would be great. And I know that Blackie and his friends will look into this, including Blackie's father. I never thought of those two ladies. And I should have." Arlyn walked away from his family, a frown on his face. There was something in the yard and he was determined to find out what it was.

Joe ran after him, a hand stopping him in his tracks.

—

"Inside, Arlyn, and now!" Joe barked at Arlyn as he spun him around and shoved him back towards the house. "Get inside, all of you." Joe watched as the men moved inside, knowing full well that Arlyn would plant himself where he could watch out of a window.

Joe watched the package closely. He had a bad feeling about it. He backed away from it as it began to click before he turned to run. He didn't make it very far when the box exploded, sending Joe flying through the air, his arms and legs waving before he hit the ground and laid in a sprawled heap. He didn't move after that.

The four men in the apartment were out of the building and running towards Joe, Cayce dropping to his knees beside their friend. Joe was struggling to regain his breath, a hand finding its way to rest on his chest. He gave a slight nod at Cayce's question if he was okay.

The other three men stared between Joe and the smoking, burning pile of a box. They had no idea what had just happened, other than that Joe had been hurt. Joe sat up, a hand to his chest as he breathed deeply. Ardan headed back for the apartment, his arms out to hug Bessie before he shoved the two ladies inside. He walked towards Skylor and sat beside her. He frowned. With all the commotion outside, he was sure that she would have been on her feet and with his wife and sister. That had not happened.

"Skylor?" Ardan tilted his head to study her.

Skylor roused to a certain degree and with that, she was on her feet, heading for her bedroom. The door closed quietly behind her.

The three older adults stood and watched in amazement and worry that she had done this. They had expected a different reaction from her.

"Did she just do that?" Bessie moved to where she could touch the bedroom door.

"She did, Bessie." Anna sighed. "She shuts down. This is likely how she has reacted all of her life, just to protect herself. She hasn't said a lot but I can only imagine how her life was."

Bessie blinked to clear her eyes from tears. Ardan's arm was around his wife, his eyes on his sister.

"We need to find someone for her to speak with." Ardan's phone was out as he moved away from his wife. A couple of text messages were sent with quick responses. The two ladies were willing to come to them and speak with Skylor. They would be there the next day and it would be up to Skylor if she wanted to talk with them that day or at a later time. Ardan tucked his phone away. He just prayed for the lady who had become so important to his son. He knew that God was in control and protecting the couple. He just wished that his son didn't have to face danger in his quest to protect the lady.

Chapter 17

Lying awake early the next morning, Skylor stared at the wall beside the bed. It was dark enough that she could not see the light sage walls but she knew the colour. It was a colour that she loved and was grateful to have it in the apartment. She was afraid, she had to acknowledge to herself and also to her Heavenly Father. She knew that He was protecting her. Skylor just didn't think that He was doing a very good job of it. She sighed and prayed for forgiveness for doubting God.

An hour later, she was on her feet, dressed and moving through the dark apartment to the kitchen. Switching on a low light, she set the kettle to boil and reached for bread to make toast. She was afraid that morning, not sure what was happening but sure that something horrible was about to happen.

Skylor moved to stand outside after her meal was complete, staring at the backyard and where her assault had happened. She had been meant to die, she decided, and shuddered at that thought. She was afraid, more afraid than when she had been under her father's care. Skylor didn't understand that because she had escaped and shamed him, he was looking for her. Once he found her, he intended to drag her back to his home and then kill her. She was leaving him very little option, he had decided. Skylor turned as she heard a soft sound and looked around before she felt something brush her ankle. She jumped and screamed, pain

---

momentarily covering her face as she felt the pain from her beating.

A little gray tabby kitten stood up at her leg, tapping a tiny white paw against her before the kitten decided just to climb up to her arms. Skylor's face softened as she cuddled the kitten close to herself and then turned to walk back into the apartment. She didn't see the men who were moving in on her and stopped short, frustrated that they were not able to take her into their custody that morning.

Skylor paced her home, the kitten cuddled close to her. She could feel and hear the purring that was shaking the little body.

"What am I to do with you?" Skylor's slim forefinger stroked the kitten's head. "I don't know if I can keep you but I want to. You need me and I need you."

Arlyn was on his feet as he heard Skylor's scream, reaching to dress readily and then ran for the backyard. He didn't see Skylor and that frightened him. He was certain that she had screamed. He searched the yards as best as he could in the dark before he ran towards her apartment door and tapped quietly.

Skylor jumped and just barely contained her scream at the tapping at her door. She crept that way, the kitten held tightly in her arms. Hearing Arlyn's voice, she drew in a deep breath. What was he doing down here at that time of the morning? She didn't want to see anyone. Skylor just wanted to be left on her own.

"Skylor?" Arlyn tapped at the door again. "Are you there?" He stood back as he heard the lock turn and the door partially open.

Skylor didn't look at Arlyn. She just couldn't. She felt too ashamed and frightened to trust anyone.

"Skylor?" Arlyn's hands gently moved her back into the apartment before he entered and closed the door behind him. A frown crossed his face as he saw the kitten peeking at him over Skylor's arm. "Are you okay?" He waited patiently for her to respond.

Skylor gave a little nod, not looking up at the tall man who stood staring down at her, worry on his face and with a prayer for her rising from his heart.

"Who's your friend?" Arlyn's finger reached out to gently touch the kitten's head.

"I found her. Is it okay if I keep her? I'll put her outside again." Skylor moved to walk past him, intent on doing just that. Only she was too scared to open the door. Someone was out there and meant her harm.

Arlyn frowned as his hand reached out to stop her forward motion. He turned slightly as he studied the door.

"No, it's okay. Stay inside." Arlyn was back outside and up to his home, retrieving a flashlight. He walked the yard again, the beam from the flashlight shining brightly as he searched for anything that was off. The light hit the multiple footprints in the dew and he sighed. Someone had been around and that meant that Skylor had likely just missed disappearing again.

—

His phone was out as he made the call that he really didn't want to make.

Skylor stood in her doorway, watching the activity around her home not that much later. She clung to the kitten, not feeling Arlyn's arm around her. She also didn't realize that she was leaning against him, finding comfort in his strength.

"Skylor? Did you see anyone this morning?" Joe stood in front of her, frustrated that she was not looking at him or responding to his questions.

Skylor just turned and walked away, heading for her bedroom. She shut the door behind her, dropping to the bed, the kitten licking at her chin. She brushed at the tears that appeared on her cheeks. Skylor never cried but here she was crying. She wrapped the kitten tighter in her arms as she sobbed. Years of repressed fear and sorrow and anger were coming out in a one great rush.

Arlyn watched her walk away even as he heard Joe muttering beside him.

"Did she just do that?" Joe stepped to where he could see the bedroom door.

"She did, Joe. She's beginning to break under everything." Arlyn sighed. "We've reached out to a couple of friends who were abused by either a parent or a foster father. They're willing to talk with her. I need to discuss that with her."

"You do? That might well help her." Joe walked away at last. He was frustrated, to say the least. He had no idea who was after Arlyn or if it really was Skylor's father after her.

Arlyn walked away as well, heading for his office. It was early, he knew, and a Saturday at that but he was troubled about something that had happened that week. He had been out where he had tracked the hawk but had found no evidence that it was there or had been for a while. The trail cams that he had installed picked up other activity but not the hawk.

Standing and staring at the video stream as he searched for the hawk, Arlyn's thoughts were muddled. He knew that he had to work but he only wanted to be with Skylor. He sat at last, reaching to pull up his email program. His work email had a number of emails but the second one that he read had him sitting back in shock. He read it over and over before he reached to send it off to Joe. On his feet, Arlyn paced his office. Who had threatened him in that way? Who wanted him dead?

Joe reached for his phone, pulling up the email. His face paled and then grew stern. He was on his feet, heading for the crime lab, forwarding them the email. He simply demanded that they find the sender, if they could. The techs shared a look and then nodded. They would do what they could but Joe realized that the possibility of finding the sender was not great.

Chapter 18

Four hours later, Arlyn was on his feet. He stretched and then twisted his wrist to stare at his watch. It was noon but felt so much later. He locked up the office and walked around his house, his thoughts troubled. He had no idea what had happened that morning but God had protected Skylor, of that he was certain.

Staring at Skylor as she appeared in front of him, Arlyn began to smile. The little kitten was still in her arms, sound asleep. He wondered if she had even set the little one down. Somehow, he doubted that.

"Skylor? How's your kitten?" Arlyn waited patiently for Skylor to respond, knowing that she would when she felt she was able to.

"I can't keep her. I need to give her away. Arlyn will never let me have her." Skylor's voice was full of sorrow. She had always wanted a gray tabby cat but had never been allowed any animals at all.

"Arlyn will let you keep her." Arlyn watched carefully as Skylor heard his words and then understood them. "Come on, love. Let's head to the local pet store. Your little one needs some gear. What will you name her?" He directed her to his truck, helping her in, an amused look on his face as she protected the kitten as best as she could.

"I can? Oh, thank you." Skylor's voice was barely audible.

"You are welcome. You need this, Skylor, more than you realize. I doubt that you've ever had a pet. That changes today. What are you going to call her?" Arlyn parked in front of the pet store, twisting on his seat to watch the lady whom he was beginning to love.

"Kayleigh. It suits her." Skylor looked up at last.

Arlyn could see the tiny crack in her demeanour that warmed his heart. Having a kitten would do her good, he decided. He wished that he had thought of that but God had stepped in once more with Skylor.

Skylor wandered the pet store, not sure what all she needed to purchase. She drew in a deep breath. She couldn't purchase anything as she had no money. Skylor turned to walk out of the store, stopping as Arlyn stepped in front of her.

"Don't worry, Skylor. We'll buy what you need. I understand that you don't have any money. It's okay. I'll buy it for you." Arlyn saw the relief on her face before she shuttered her face.

Arlyn's neck tingled as he raised his head. He looked around, knowing that someone was watching them. He just couldn't decide who it was.

Joe watched as Skylor walked towards him, a frown on her face. He sighed. He needed to talk with her about what had happened that morning. It just didn't look as if that was going to happen.

"Skylor? What happened this morning?" Joe stepped into her path, refusing to let her pass him. "And just what are you holding?"

"A kitten. And I don't know anything about what happened this morning. The only thing that I saw was Kayleigh." She moved around him and entered her apartment, the door shutting quietly behind her.

"Did she just do that again?" Joe was frustrated at how often Skylor was avoiding him. "She can't keep doing that."

"Lighten up, Joe." Cayce stood on one side of him, Briar on the other. Their parents and aunt stood behind them. "She's not your normal victim. She has been kept isolated and suppressed for almost thirty years. That's right. Thirty years. Aunt Anna found out that her birthday is next week. Do you know that she has never celebrated it? She has not celebrated anything that we normally do and take for granted? How is she supposed to feel?" Cayce's voice was heated. "She has no idea how to live. That's up to us to teach her how to live."

Joe's head had turned as Cayce spoke. He had forgotten that. He had just become so wrapped up in the investigation and that of Arlyn's that he had lost sight of her as a human being and as an individual.

"You're right, Cayce. Forgive me. I'm just so worried about her and Arlyn and frustrated that this is going nowhere." Joe walked away, needing to be on another crime scene. He didn't like to walk away, though, with unfinished business and a talk that really needed to happen.

Arlyn had stayed in the background as Cayce told Joe off. He knew that Cayce was speaking to Joe

—

as a friend. He walked forward to lay a hand on Cayce's shoulders.

"Mom? Aunt Anna? Would you please check on Skylor? And she does have a kitten that needs to be looked after." Arlyn had set all their purchases into the apartment just as Joe had appeared.

Anna and Bessie shared a look before they both hugged Arlyn and moved past him into the apartment. They shared another look as they couldn't find Skylor in the living room. Soft muttering could be heard from the kitchen, drawing them that way. They stood, watching as Skylor sat cross-legged on the floor, the kitten playing around her.

"Skylor? Who's this?" Bessie sat near to the younger lady, drawing the attention of the kitten.

"Kayleigh. I found her this morning." Skylor looked up, tears on her face. "I can't afford to keep her but so help me, I need her. Arlyn spent all that money on her this morning. I can't repay him." Skylor was talking very rapidly, her words almost inaudible.

"Skylor?" Bessie waited for Skylor to look at her. Her heart was breaking for the young lady who had claimed her son's heart. Bessie didn't need to be told that. She could tell that fact by how Arlyn was treating Skylor. "It's okay. He can afford whatever your kitten needs. And whatever you need. He's looking after you, Skylor, being the hands and feet of Christ on earth."

Skylor stared at Bessie and then up at Anna, who handed her a warm damp cloth. She was nodding in agreement. None of the ladies heard the door open quietly and then shut just as quietly. Arlyn had appeared, hearing the conversation between his mother and his lady. He drew in a sad breath, knowing that he had to talk to Skylor. He dropped to the floor beside her, an arm around her.

Jumping as she felt Arlyn hugging her, Skylor turned her head, finding herself nose to nose with him. She frowned at the look in his eyes, a look that said that she was precious and lovable and that he would do everything he could to protect her.

Chapter 19

To say that Joe was frustrated would be an understatement. He hurt from the blast earlier that day. He had walked away from Arlyn and Skylor without any answers. And Joe was very much worried about the couple. And they were a couple, Joe acknowledged. He looked up at the sky as he stood beside his car, praying for his friends.

Briar and Cayce walked around the yard, stopping at the burned area in the front yard. They were thankful that no one had been hurt but were deeply puzzled by the blast. There hadn't been anything left of the box or whatever the container had been.

"What is going on, Briar?" Cayce was puzzled at the events. "Which one was the target?"

"We don't know that, Cayce. And I wish we did. I fear for Arlyn and Skylor." Briar turned to face the house, a frown on his face before he stalked towards the door that led to Arlyn's office. He yanked off the piece of paper, something that seemed to have appeared while they were all out there. "What is this?"

Cayce had paced beside him, leaning over to read the threat that was contained on the page.

"This goes with that box." He looked around, seeing Joe watching them. He waved for Joe to join then, hearing Arlyn's footsteps as he approached.

"Briar? What is that?" Arlyn reached and took the paper from between his brother's fingers. He could hear the birds that he loved singing around him. It just seemed so surreal. He read the words, not quite taking in what they were saying. He felt the page taken from him and then the angry words spoken around him.

Joe's hand on Arlyn's back shoved him towards his home and then inside. The door was closed and locked behind them, Ardan appearing at the sound of the heavy footsteps.

"What is going on, Joe?" Ardan stopped the officer with a hand on his arm. "What is that?" He pointed at the paper.

"A death threat, Ardan, against Arlyn and Skylor. I want to know who is behind this. And we don't have enough information to determine just who or why." Joe paced, frustration evident on his face.

"We'll make it a deeper matter of prayer, Joe." Ardan nodded at his three sons. "And God is in control. It is in His timing that we determine who and why. We pray for protection for Arlyn and Skylor. We have had friends go through danger who survived. It changes a person but it is in God's will. It is hard to wait for Him to work, but it's what we must do." He walked away, the front door closing quietly behind him.

Arlyn stared after his father, knowing how heavy his heart would be. He sighed to himself. Turning back to his brothers, he saw the concern on their faces and the fear that they were trying had to hide.

"Guys? What are we to do?" Arlyn ran his hands through his hair. He was at a loss as to what to do but he needed to work. He walked through to his office, shutting that door behind him and shutting him inside the office.

Skylor came looking for him a few hours later, the kitten asleep in her arms. She just had trouble letting go of her furry companion.

Arlyn looked up and then was on his feet to reach for Skylor. He swept her into a hug and then prayed for her. He didn't know if his prayers were working but that was all that he could do for her. He could not step in and protect her, not in the way that he wanted to.

"Arlyn? What was that all about?" Skylor's voice was low and hesitant, almost as if she was afraid to ask him anything. Asking any questions had always earned her a beating and she had just stopped asking anything.

"The bomb? The letter? It was a threat against me, Skylor. And we don't know why." Arlyn was frustrated at that. His enemies had threatened to start reaching out to his family and he wanted to save them from that at any cost.

"A threat? To kill you?" Skylor leaned back at last and looked up at him, fear on her face as she did so that he would punish her for being bold.

"Yes. And they mention you. Not by name but as my lady." Arlyn bit at his lip, staring at the window in front of him.

"Your lady? Oh, no! I'm not that!" Skylor was shocked at his words. "That will never happen."

"But it could, Skylor. It really could. I am falling in love with you, sweetheart. I don't know if you will ever love me. But that doesn't change that I will do everything in my power and with God's help to protect you and find your father and his cronies and bring them to justice. That is my promise." Arlyn refused to look down at her, not wanting to see her rejection of him on her face.

Skylor stared up at him, remembering at last to close her mouth. She felt Kayleigh stirring in her arms and hugged the kitten tighter. Did Arlyn really mean that? Did he really say that he was falling in love with her? It had been her prayer for years for a knight to walk in and free her. Arlyn had started that process of allowing her to find her freedom and her faith and to grow as a lady should.

"Do you mean that, Arlyn? No one has ever said that to me." She snorted, bringing a grin to his face and startling Kayleigh for a moment.

"I do, sweetheart. I really do." Arlyn looked down at the lady who he held. "I want to see where our friendship goes but it has to be at a pace that is comfortable for you."

"Thank you, Arlyn. Now, what do we need to do right now?" Skylor pushed away from him and walked to the desk that she had been using. She set the kitten down on the desktop and Kayleigh immediately began to explore it. A soft smile lit Skylor's face, bringing out her beauty.

"We were trying to determine if there are any people out there who are after me and after black market birds. I think that there are, and I have come onto their radar. I just don't know how to track that."

"We'll figure it out. I don't know anything about computers but is there a way to track them?"

"There is." Arlyn gave her another quick hug. "I have a friend who can help."

Chapter 20

Skylor ran for the apartment door the next morning. She had been wandering the yard and had arrived at the back of it, to stand and draw in a deep breath of the fresh morning air. She then turned to study the woods backing the yard. Hearing a noise, Skylor had spun and then began to run towards the house, fear lending speed to her feet.

Slamming the door behind her and locking it, Skylor slid to the floor, her back to the door. She couldn't say that she heard anyone running after her. Her heart beat had been too loud for her to hear anyone. Even if there hadn't been, whoever it was had driven her to deep terror. Skylor reached for Kayleigh as she climbed and tumbled over her, her purrs sounding loud in the silence.

Arlyn had barely caught a glimpse of Skylor racing for her home before he was out of the house and stalking towards the end of the yard. He searched without finding anything, stopping suddenly as he heard the call of a bird. His head tilted and his focus changed from searching to listening. His face lit up with pleasure. It was a cardinal, one of his most favourite birds. He turned to face the house, sighing.

Working through the stack of requests to speak that littered his desk, Arlyn finally rose and stretched. A glance at his watch let him know that it was close to lunchtime. He locked up his office and headed for the apartment door, tapping softly. He frowned as he didn't receive an answer from Skylor. Pulling out his phone, he searched his text messages, a grin covering his face as he found the message from his parents, simply stating that if he wanted to join them for lunch, they and Skylor would be at their favourite diner. Arlyn ran for his truck and drove away, not watching the truck that pulled out behind him and followed him. This lack of attention would be something that would come back to haunt him in the coming days.

Skylor looked up as she felt an arm around her and slid over on the seat. Her face didn't really open up but her eyes showed her happiness at seeing Arlyn. Ardan and Bessie shared a look, both nodding. It was obvious that there was interest on Skylor's part but they both knew that it would take time and prayer for Skylor to open up to Arlyn.

Arlyn dropped a kiss on Skylor's temple without thinking about his action and then turned to greet his parents. He didn't see the shocked look that covered her face before it softened. He was reaching through into her heart and she was realizing at last that she was a person of value, particularly of value to God.

Skylor watched as Arlyn interacted with his parents. Sadness grew in her heart that she had never had that closeness with her father. She never understood why he had acted as he had. She looked up as Arlyn touch her hand.

"Dad asked if you were okay." Arlyn waited for her to speak.

"I don't know, Arlyn. Ardan? How do I know how to feel? This is all so strange." Skylor blinked at them, her thoughts muddled.

"That's understandable, Skylor. You have never known a life that has been free from abuse. You're learning now that you have choices and freedom. It is difficult to trust others, not having that contact with them. We want to help you become the lady who you should and could be." Ardan nodded at Arlyn. "I don't know if you two will ever be a couple. That's up to God and you two. For now, trust Arlyn to be in your life. He will protect you as best he can. We all will. We love you as a daughter already, Skylor. We always wanted a daughter but God chose otherwise for us. We're fine with that. When the boys marry, their ladies will be our daughters." Ardan paused for a moment. "Keep doing what you're doing. Pray through everything. Spend time with God in prayer and in study of the scriptures. If you want to study with anyone, Bessie or Anna will be glad to do that with you. We have two ladies who are friends who both had abusive foster fathers. They would like to tell you their stories, if you want to hear them."

"You do? Oh! How I would! Do you know what it was like to be so isolated, so put down, so abused to the point where you have no self respect and that no one cares about you. I just don't understand why, And I don't know if he's chasing me or not. Would he have tracked me?" Skylor jumped as Arlyn's hand grasped hers. "Arlyn?"

"Skylor? Did we ever search your belongings and shoes for any tracking devices?"

Skylor shrugged. She had no idea if they had or not. She really had no idea what a tracker was.

"I have no idea what that is. Can you explain it please?" Skylor kept her eyes on the tabletop.

"A tracker is something that shows someone where you are. They don't have to be in the same city as you. They can follow you as the signal would go to a computer program." Arlyn patiently explained it to her.

Skylor was horrified. She stuttered as she tried to speak, knowing that was exactly what her father would have done.

"He would do that. I don't understand how the door was unlocked. It was never unlocked. Did he do that on purpose?"

"He might have." Bessie shared a look with Arlyn. "We have a friend who is a private investigator. When he heard about you, he started a preliminary investigation. He wants to speak with you. In fact, one of the ladies who would like to share their story is his daughter-in-law."

"She is? He did? Oh, I can't pay him. I don't have any money." Skylor was in tears at the thought. She jumped once more as Arlyn's hand tightened on hers.

"He won't charge you anything, Skylor. He doesn't for friends. It's how he is. In fact, I would suspect that he and his wife will come with Blackie and Julia if you want to speak with them." Arlyn shared a look with his father. "As to money, I will pay you to work in my office. This is what you can expect." Skylor stared at him in shock at the number that he said, leaving Arlyn to reach and give her a hug.

"I do. I want this over. You need to go on with your life and you can't while you're stuck with me." Skylor was lost in thought, a sober look on her face. She didn't see the look that crossed Arlyn's face, one that almost broke his parents' hearts.

"It's okay, Skylor. I am where God wants me for now." Arlyn reached to hug her, finding her leaning against him. He frowned at that. Usually, she just kept her body stiff.

Chapter 21

Opening the front door to his house that afternoon, Arlyn's face lit up. Blackie and Julia stood there, the lady reaching to hug him. Samuel and Miriam just moved in on him as well. The two couples walked into his kitchen, greeting Ardan and Bessie. They then turned to Skylor, finding her backed up to Arlyn and staring at the floor. Julia shared a look with Blackie before she moved to stand in front of Skylor.

"This is Skylor? That's a beautiful name. I'm Julia and I think that we need to talk. God told me that I have a story to share with you." Julia waited patiently for Skylor to react, knowing how she had felt when Blackie and his friends had walked in and saved her.

"You do?" Skylor scraped together her courage to look up, sure that she would see censure and hatred on the lady's face. Instead, she saw compassion and friendship. She really didn't know how to react. She had never faced the acceptance and love that she had in the last few weeks.

"I do. Now, where can we talk?" Julia reached carefully to hug Skylor, seeing Arlyn stepping back as she did so. He nodded in thanks as he did so. Julie just turned Skylor towards the living room, hearing Miriam and Bessie following them. She seated them on the couch even as the men's voices reached to them. "Talk to me as you want to and can, Skylor. Arlyn has given the basics."

Skylor shrugged, not sure what to say. She looked up under her lashes and saw the two older ladies watching her. She somehow knew that they were praying for her and for that she was grateful. She had not been aware of anyone praying for her in the past.

"I don't know what to say. I had no life. My father kept me locked in the house all of my life. I had no contact with anyone else that I can remember. If he wasn't home, I was locked in my bedroom. There were bars on the windows that kept me from escaping. I used to try. I guess that I just gave up."

"That's normal, Skylor. I did the same. My mother had my father killed and then remarried to the police chief. He was brutal and abusive. He was in on my father's murder. I had a very shabby bedroom and attached bath even though the rest of the house was almost opulent in appearance. Blackie and his friends stepped in to help me. My mother had chased my brother away when he was just a teen. We lost touch for years until after Blackie started helping me. I didn't know at the time that he worked for Samuel." Julia bit at her lip. "You may never have heard of the town of Mistletoe. What Blackie and I went through and what his three friends and their wives went through went back to the founding families. There were five and we are descendants of them all. My mother and her husband thought that they could force me to sign over my share of the inheritance from the town. I refused and that's when my life became more brutal." Julia paused at that, reliving the horror of her earlier life.

"You are? They did?" Skylor looked up at the ceiling, seeking reassurance and peace from God. She found that, which didn't surprise her any more. She knew that she had people praying for her, people whom she had never met and might never meet. "I don't think I have an inheritance that I should be receiving." She looked around in fear for a moment as she heard an unknown voice speak.

Samuel had listened to Julia and then to Skylor. He had done some research as had Blackie. A friend of Blackie's, Simon, had started a search on Skylor, not liking what he was finding. He led the department that searched for missing children, his wife, Eavan, a long-lost sister to Julia who had been abandoned by their mother as a newborn.

"We have been looking into you and your family, Skylor." Samuel gave a smile as Skylor's head shot around and she stared at him in fright. "Don't be afraid, Skylor. No one will know where you are from us. We take great care in protecting anyone whom we are investigating. Now, what can we do for you?"

"Do for you? I'm sorry. I don't understand. I don't need anything done for me. I never had. I'm not worth that." Skylor's facial expression did not change as she spoke. Those were the words that she had heard ever since she could remember.

"You are worth it, Skylor." Blackie spoke up at that. He shared a look with Julia. She had felt the same and at times even now she had to be reminded that she was worth it to God and to Blackie and his family and their friends. "We understand to a certain extent why you would say that. That's all you've ever heard. God loved you so much that He sent his Son to die to redeem you. He knew the path that you would walk from before time began. He provided friends to help you. We would like to be considered friends of yours, if you would allow us that. You were bought with a price that can never have an amount put on it." He gave her a smile and saw her tremulous one in return.

"Thank you. No one has ever helped me until I came here. I just don't understand though. Why me?" Skylor was shifted over on the couch as Arlyn found a seat beside her and wrapped an arm round her. She stared up at him for a moment, not realizing that he was staking his claim to her in front of the others and not seeing them nodding in return.

"That's what we're working on. Did you ever suspect that your father was not your father?" Samuel spoke up once more, sharing a look with Blackie. That was one thought that Simon had been working on.

Skylor shrugged. To tell the truth, she had wondered at that but had not thought of that in many years. She just was grateful to be free from him. She just wanted to forget him and her life but knew that was impossible. Her life had made her into the person that she was.

"I thought of that when I was a child and wanted answers. I never got them. I guess that I just gave up." Skylor relaxed back against Arlyn, feeling safe with him. This was new to her, she decided. "I feel safe here. I never felt safe at my father's home."

"No, I don't suspect that you would." Blackie looked around as he heard footsteps and waved at Cayce, Briar, and Joe as they appeared. "We will do everything that we can to protect you. Unfortunately, our best might not be enough."

———

115

Skylor nodded, knowing that Blackie was speaking the truth. She had come to the conclusion that no one could really protect her.

Joe took the folders that he was handed, taking the time to read through them. He was not surprised at the conclusions that Samuel and the others had come to. He would need to prove their conclusions but he would do that. For today, thought, he was off duty and here as a friend to both Skylor and Arlyn. Joe frowned at a thought. What if the two were connected in a way that they had not considered? What if the man claiming to be Skylor's father was involved in black market shipments and those shipments were the birds that Arlyn was protecting? He sent off a quick text to his friend in Skylor's town and asked that very question.

Chapter 22

Skylor had listened to the information that Samuel and Blackie gave her. She was just too overwhelmed, she decided, and just too tired to take it all in. The event that had happened a few days ago had drained her physically and mentally. Skylor looked over at Blackie, a frown on her face.

"What are you saying here? I'm sorry. I don't really understand any of it."

"That's okay, Skylor. We understand it to some degree because it is what we do. However, for you, it's all brand new. You will need to read the material over and over. We are available at any time to speak with you." Blackie was adamant on that.

"Thank you. Are you certain about my father? That's he's not that?" Skylor was beginning to see some light in it all. "He never acted like one. If I weren't, that would explain why he hid me away."

"Even if you were his, he hid you for a reason. We've been speaking with your former neighbours. None of them knew that you were there. If they had, they all have said that they would have reported it to child protection services or to the police. They would have ensured that you got out of the house." Samuel had personally spoken with these people. All had been horrified to have heard of the life that Skylor had led.

"I see." Skylor suddenly yawned, her face turning into Arlyn's shoulder as she slept. Kayleigh snuggled up near her neck, her purr sounding loud in the silence.

"She's not recovered from the other day yet." Bessie shook her head. "She'll be embarrassed that she went to sleep. She just doesn't know how to act or what to say so she stays quiet or just walks away."

"She'll do that, Bessie." Julia prayed for her new friend. "I still do at times. You know my story. I had nothing like this that Skylor faced. And neither does Eavan. We need to Eavan and Simon here to talk with you, Arlyn."

"And we will. We just need to watch that we don't overwhelm her. And it's a hard balance to know when that happens. She hides everything, just because of how that man treated her." Arlyn looked over at Joe. "Joe? Aren't you working today?"

Joe shook his head.

"Not today. I'm off for the next couple of days but I will continue to work on what you have found. Now, you have another friend who could speak with Skylor?"

"We do. Rachel and Timothy. And Gideon, Rachel's brother. They were in a foster home where the foster parents abused them. Gideon was locked out of the house when he was eighteen before he was beaten and dropped in a town miles from their home town. Rachel did run for a while. What she didn't know was that Gideon was heading back to find her when she turned eighteen. He's also a private investigator." Arlyn's head went back. "Joe, we know someone who would willingly help. We need to reach out to her."

"Do that. For now, we need to pray for you both." Joe was as good as his words as his head bent and he began to pray for Arlyn and Skylor, his prayer taken up by those in the room.

A few hours later, Arlyn stood and stared down at Skylor. She had not awakened and he had not had the heart to do that. An arm rested across his shoulders as Briar stood beside him.

"How are you hanging on, Arlyn?"

Arlyn shrugged. He had no idea how to feel. He watched his lady as she slept, his mother and aunt sitting nearby.

"I don't know, Briar." He sighed. "I need to do some work and I don't want to."

Briar turned his brother towards the office and shoved him that way.

"Let me see what I can do to help you. You're needing to be out in the field again."

"I am. And I don't feel safe. Skylor will want to be out there with me. How do I do this?" Arlyn sank into his chair, his head resting in his hands. He was totally discouraged that day.

"Let's see what friends of ours can help. I know that we can't have a lot of us out there." Briar looked around for a moment. "Joe might be able to come up with some officers who might be willing to go out there with you."

———

"That's a thought. I'll reach out to him. For now though, I could use some help. What are your thoughts on black market?" Arlyn shoved a folder across the desk towards Briar. "Read this and then let me know your thoughts."

Briar studied his brother for a moment, seeing the stress that Arlyn was under. He sighed and then began to pray for his brother, begging God to end this whatever it was and keep his brother and his lady safe. His eyes dropped to the folder as he began to read.

There was silence in the building as both brothers worked through the information. Cayce appeared at some point, taking the pages that Briar was handing over to him. He too studied his brother before he was on his feet, walking around inside the building. He studied the birds that Briar had worked on for his brother through his taxidermist business. His attention then went to the photos. He paused in front of one, a frown on his face.

"Arlyn? This is a new photo, isn't it?" He turned to find his brother rising and walking towards him.

"It is. I took it about a month ago. Why?" Arlyn frowned at his brother, not sure what was going on.

"There. In the background. Did you see that face?" Cayce's finger stabbed at the photo, hitting the glass of the frame.

"What?" Arlyn stared at the photo, not seeing what Cayce had seen. "I don't see anything, Cayce."

"There. Near that oak tree. Someone is watching you." Cayce's finger hit the glass once more. "Don't you see it?"

Arlyn shook his head. He was not seeing what Cayce was seeing. Cayce shoved Arlyn's face closer to the photo. Arlyn then drew in a deep breath. He could see what Cayce was seeing. He didn't know the man who was hidden in the trees.

"Him? I never saw that before." Arlyn rubbed at his face. "We need to call Joe."

"And we will." Cayce removed the photo and then shoved Arlyn towards the door. "Lock up, Arlyn. We need to find your lady."

Chapter 23

Skylor looked at the photo, seeing the man that Cayce was pointing out. She frowned. She had no idea who that man was.

"Who is that?" Skylor looked at Cayce and then at Arlyn.

"We don't know. I never saw it until now." Arlyn was distraught at that. He should have seen the man but his focus had been on the birds in the photo instead.

"It's okay, Arlyn. It's okay." Skylor looked around as she heard footsteps. "Joe? There's a man in this photo." She thrust the photo towards him.

Joe almost dropped the photo. Skylor had shoved it at him so quickly that he barely had a chance to grab it.

"What are you talking about?" Joe stared at the three in front of them, seeing Briar approaching as well.

"There. In the photo. A man in the shadows." Skylor leaned against him for a moment as her finger pointed out the figure.

"I see." Joe studied the man, recognizing him from a wanted poster that had just crossed his desk. "Arlyn? When did you take this photo?"

"That photo? Six months ago, I think. I know it wasn't recently. I can check the copies on my computer." Arlyn was puzzled. "Why would he be there?"

"That's what we need to find out. He is wanted in many cities, Arlyn, for many crimes, not the least of which is murder. If he was stalking you, then you are in true danger. How do we keep you safe? And how do we keep Skylor safe? He'll go after her to get to you. That makes what is happening to Skylor doubly dangerous."

"We get that, Joe." Arlyn sighed. This was not how the day was to go, he decided. "How do we do this?" He didn't think that there was an easy answer to that question.

"That I don't know, Arlyn. We can come up with plans but those plans may not work." Joe walked away, the photo clutched in his hand.

Arlyn watched him walk away before he turned to the group that was standing behind him. He shrugged before he lifted up his hands.

"I have no idea what to do. Do any of you?"

They all shared a look before Briar nodded. He pointed towards the kitchen.

"We have food that we need to eat. Then, we'll pray. And then, Skylor will share her thoughts with us." He grinned as she stared at him, before she frowned.

Two hours later, Skylor stared at Briar. It had become a staring contest between them. It had surprised all of them as she had never done this before. Arlyn had a slight smile on his face as he tried to figure out which one of them would win the staring contest. He was glad to see Skylor beginning to open up. He turned his attention to Cayce, who sat with a wide smile on his face. Cayce shrugged as he read his brother's thoughts.

"Skylor? What are you thinking?" Joe finally broke through the silence in the room.

"What am I thinking?" Skylor's hands flew up into the air. "What am I thinking? I have no idea what I am to think. I've never been allowed to have any thoughts of my own." Her words were spit out in anger. This reaction was not what they had expected from her.

"I have no idea, Skylor. Just start talking to us." Joe grinned at her, holding up his pen. He had never left the house, just walked away to make some calls. "I'll take notes."

"You're not a secretary, Joe. You're an investigator." Skylor could barely sit. It was only Arlyn's arm around her shoulders that kept her in her chair.

"It's what I do, Skylor. I take notes. I know that we have gone over and over what you have lived. Have you remembered anything else?" Joe waited patiently for Skylor to respond.

Arlyn tilted his head to watch her. He wasn't sure if she would say anything or not. He prayed for her, knowing that she needed to talk but he wasn't sure if she would.

———

Skylor's eyes dropped to the table top. She was ashamed of her outburst, not realizing that it was just okay if she responded like that. Skylor had been severely disciplined if she had spoken up for herself. It had become ingrained in her not to respond.

"It's okay, Skylor." Arlyn's arm tightened around her. "It's okay to be angry. It's part of who we are as people. God understands your anger."

Skylor blinked at him, not sure if what he was saying was the truth. Anger in her life had been directed at her in a physical way, leading to many beatings that she didn't deserve.

"I didn't know that, Arlyn. I am just so angry. I'm angry at my father. I'm angry at my life. I'm angry at whoever it is that is doing this to us. And I am angry at God. And I shouldn't be."

"It's okay to be angry, Skylor. God understands that you're angry and He knows the full reason why. All you have to do is ask for His forgiveness. It's freely given. Now, can we start writing down what your thoughts are?"

Skylor shrugged. She had begun to freeze up again, not willing to speak. Her life up to that point was something that she didn't want to go back and live through again. And that was exactly what she was being asked to do. She was on her feet, shoving away from Arlyn and running for her apartment. The door was closed and locked behind her as she stood in the kitchen. Skylor wanted to run and run as far from here as she could. She just didn't think that Arlyn would let her. And that frightened her. Skylor wasn't sure which one of them was the target. She was certain that it was her but the photo stated otherwise.

Arlyn had risen to his feet as Skylor had fled. And she was in flight. He had seen that in nature too many times not to recognize it. He sighed before he found his seat again. His eyes were on his father, seeing the compassion in his father's eyes.

"Joe? What can you tell us about this man?" Bessie reached the photo, studying it before she pointed to another area. "There's another man in the photo, Joe."

"What?" Joe reached for the photo once more and sighed. Bessie was correct. There were two men in the photo. "Arlyn? What did you go and do?"

Arlyn stared at him. He had no idea what he had done, other than his work.

"I have no idea, Joe. All I was doing that day was searching for that hawk and then taking notes about it. Is that a crime?" Arlyn's head dropped as he drew in a deep breath. He wanted this over but it certainly didn't seem that it would be soon.

Chapter 24

The next day, Arlyn paced through the woods near his home. He was on a search for a certain bird but couldn't find the pair or even hear them. He knew where they usually nested and cautiously approached it. Waiting patiently for the birds to appear, he frowned. Finally, Arlyn reached up to peer into the nest. It was empty and looked as if it had not been used that year. And that was strange. That pair of birds were always there.

Dropping back from his tiptoes, Arlyn rubbed at the back of his neck. It was tingling as if he was being watched. He spun in a circle, not seeing anyone but that didn't matter. Someone was out there and monitoring him. Arlyn walked away at last after searching the area in expanding circles, desperate to find the birds and not finding them. Back at his truck, Arlyn paused before he jumped into his truck and drove away. Watching in his rearview mirror, he saw the car that pulled out and followed him.

Heading for the police department, Arlyn nodded as the car turned off before he arrived there. He drove on past and headed for his home. He had work to do in the office that he had been neglecting. And he wanted to find Skylor.

Skylor looked around from the desk that she had planted herself at earlier that day. She had tried to work but wasn't certain just what she was to be doing. The filing she had figured out on her own, and the mail had been opened and organized as best as she could.

Skylor knew that God was guiding her. Otherwise everything would have been a mess. She looked around as she heard the door to the house opening, fear briefly crossing her face.

Arlyn stopped for a moment before he was across the room and hugging Skylor. She hugged him back, shocked at his movements. She was finding that her emotions were becoming more free, something she had prayed for but never expected to have happen.

"Having a good day, love?" Arlyn perched on the corner of her desk, forgetting that he had planned to work.

"I have no idea. What is a good day?" Skylor's eyes dropped to the desk. "I'm sorry. I talked back. I shouldn't have done that."

Arlyn stared at her for a moment before his head dropped. He should expect these kinds of comments, he knew. They just hurt every time he heard them.

"I'm sure that you did." Arlyn looked over her desk. "You've been working."

"I have. I just don't know if I've done everything the way that you want it." Skylor bit at her lip, uncertainty on her face.

"It's okay, Skylor. You've done it the way that makes sense to you. That's what we do." Arlyn was on his feet. "I need to do some work. What can I get for you to do?"

Skylor shrugged. She held up a folder.

"I've been reading through what Joe left. I shouldn't be doing that while you're paying me to work." Skylor was ready to run and hide.

"It's okay, Skylor. You just continue reading that and making any notes that you need to." Arlyn was soon deep into his work, tossing papers to one side as he completed them. He sat back at last, staring at the mess on his desk. He sighed and began to sort through the papers, surprised to see Skylor working with him.

"The government documents, Arlyn? Do you mail them or send them some other way?" Skylor bit at her lip. She really didn't know how mail worked. And that angered her.

"It's okay, Skylor. Talk to me. Yell at me. Take out your anger on me. I can take it and help you." Arlyn reached to hug her, finding her stiff in his arms. He released her and turned to the documents that she was holding. "We can fax these in." His hand reached for hers as he tugged her to the fax machine. "I'll teach you how to do that."

Arlyn was as good as his word, showing her how to use the machine and then standing back and watching her, a soft smile on his face as she turned to him, happiness flickering on her face for once. It only made her more beautiful and took more of his heart.

"We're done, I think, for the day, love." Arlyn reached to turn off the lights and lock the door behind her. "How be I take you out for a meal?"

"It's too dangerous to do that, Arlyn." Skylor stared up at him, not sure if they should do that.

<hr>

"We need to be out and about. By going out there, we're showing that we're ready to continue to live our lives." He bit at his lip for a moment. "You are a beautiful lady with hidden depths that are beginning to show. I am proud to be your friend. I would like to date you but you're not ready for that." Arlyn watched the emotions flickering across her face.

"You do?" Skylor suddenly reached to hug him, a spontaneous movement that surprised them both. "Then, we date."

Arlyn stared at her and then began to laugh as he tucked her into his truck and then ran around the truck to jump behind the wheel. He drove off, watching the same car behind them.

"We have a tail, love."

Skylor turned to look behind them, not surprised.

"That's what they do, isn't it? Trail us and then attack us." Skylor settled back in her seat. "How do we know which one of us they're after?"

"We don't. We look at it as if they are after both of us. And they are. We're both a danger to ourselves and one another. I'm not walking away from you. Not ever."

"Thank you, Arlyn. Where are we heading?" Skylor studied the area around them as he parked. "This restaurant?"

"Yes, this restaurant. You deserve the best." Arlyn reached for Skylor's hand and walked her towards the restaurant. He could hear footsteps behind him and knew that the men who had been stalking them in their car were now stalking them on foot. He prayed for protection for them.

Two hours later, Arlyn locked the front door behind him. Skylor was locked into her apartment, he knew, and was at least safe, he prayed, for the night. He stretched and then walked to his office, sitting at the desk in his home office. He pulled up his email program, reading through the emails that had come in. Arlyn paused at the email from Simon before he responded that he would like to meet with him. Tomorrow worked for him, he stated.

Night dropped down on the house, hiding the activity of the men who searched around the house for a way in. There was none. This frustrated the men. They were under increasing pressure to find a way to take Arlyn captive once more and bring him to their employer. Skylor was to be kidnapped as well but taken somewhere else, away from Arlyn. They would use the two against one another if they could.

———

Chapter 26

The next morning, Arlyn stared with horror at the debris on his front lawn. It was a mix of broken wood, car parts, and pieces of metal. He walked around it, frowning at the pile before he reached for his phone. Joe was shocked at what Arlyn had to say. He promised to be there right away. Would Arlyn and Skylor stay safe?

Skylor walked around the pile of debris as well, a thoughtful look on her face. The debris reminded her of her father who had been in the junk business, particularly metal and vehicles.

"This is from my father, Arlyn." She looked up at the sky. "He's found me and is threatening me. I've seen piles like this in the past."

"You have? Your father?" Arlyn wrapped an arm around her to keep her still and close to him.

"Yes. Him. He would pile stuff like this in the back yard of the house that he owned." Skylor blinked, not really focusing on what was around her. "He would do it as a threat. Only I ever knew what the threat was."

"He was trying to control you, Skylor. And he did a good job at that." Arlyn looked around as he heard a car stop. "Joe's here. He'll work through what is out here." He looked around at Joe. "Joe?"

"Arlyn? What is this?" Joe stopped the couple, eyeing them and then the pile of debris.

"I have no idea." Arlyn looked down at Skylor, finding her watching the debris pile as she expected it to move or to speak.

"When did you find it?" Joe walked around the pile, a frown in place on his face.

"Just a few moments ago. I had been busy in my home office and then Skylor appeared in the office. I didn't see it right away. And I didn't hear anything over night." Arlyn was frustrated. He should have heard something and didn't.

"I see. Give me some time. For now, head for the police tape and your family, Arlyn. They're waiting for you." Joe stared at Skylor as she was shaking her head. "Yes, Skylor. You need to head that way. You can't stay here. Go on with Arlyn." He hid a smile at the disgruntled look on her face before she turned and stalked away from him. Arlyn just gave a shrug, a smile on his own face.

Bessie and Ardan hugged the couple before they frowned at them and then looked past them at Joe.

"Son? What's going on?" Ardan finally asked the question that was burning on all of their lips.

Arlyn hesitated. He had no idea what had happened other than a pile of debris appeared on his lawn. He said as much to his father.

"A pile of debris?" Ardan was shocked at that. "Who would do that?"

"My father. He's tracked me down." Skylor didn't have any expression of emotion on her face. It was just so matter of fact for her. "He's in the junk yard business. So, it would be nothing for him to do this." She walked away from them, Cayce and Briar walking one on each side of her. Their attention was on the area around them.

Arlyn watched her walk away, knowing that she felt incredibly guilty about what had happened. He sighed. There was nothing that said that her father had been responsible for that pile of debris, despite her conviction that he was.

Joe walked towards Arlyn, watching Skylor in the distance. He nodded. Cayce and Briar would watch out for her and return her back to where Arlyn was waiting.

"Joe? What did you find?" Arlyn kept his eyes steady on Skylor as she walked back towards him.

"What did I find? Other than a pile of debris? Nothing. Absolutely nothing. That's strange, you know. Someone did this on purpose. So who did it?"

"Her father?" Arlyn reached to draw Skylor closer to him.

"That's possible. That's one person that we'll consider. Other than that, I have no idea who put that there." Joe was angry and it showed. It was not often that he showed anger, usually keeping his anger controlled.

Skylor stared at the activity surrounding the house, a frown on her face. She then cleared the frown from her face and stood there in the cooler air of the day, her face expressionless. Arlyn had watched her as the emotions had cleared from her face. He knew that this was likely a habit with her.

Joe turned as his name was called and walked rapidly towards the tech who was waving at him.

"Bill? What did you find?" Joe headed for the debris pile that the techs were sorting through and then tagging as evidence.

"This." Bill pointed to the message spray painted on the lawn. "We found this as we moved the debris."

Joe stared at him and then down at the lawn. He sighed to himself before he began to pray for his friends. He didn't like the fact that they were threatened. He had no idea why they were being threatened. He turned to look at the couple before he turned back to the tech.

"Whoever this is? They're getting bold." Joe took his own pictures. He would need to talk to the couple but for now, he was trying to think through how to keep them safe. There just didn't seem to be a way to do that.

Arlyn tightened his arm around Skylor. He could feel the faint shudders that trembled through her body. She just wasn't speaking. In fact, she had shut down as she used to do when her father threatened her.

Bessie watched Skylor carefully, knowing that she needed to reach out to the younger lady. She just didn't know how. Anna had moved to stand beside Skylor, wrapping an arm around the younger lady's. She had begun to understand Skylor and knew that the younger lady would not speak, not at that time. For now, they had to let her have her silence.

Chapter 27

Late that night, Arlyn slumped on his couch, not sure what to think or what to do. It had taken hours for the house and yard to be cleared for them to return home. No matter how much they had tried to get Skylor to leave, she just refused to. Skylor had stood at the police line for hours, not responding to any of them. They had shared looks with one another and then did what they could for her.

He rose at last, heading for his home office. He didn't think that he would sleep. Instead, he reached for his Bible. He needed that time with God, searching for the verses on justice and protection. Arlyn laid his Bible to one side after what seemed hours. He yawned and then reached to wake up his computer, searching his emails for any answers that might be waiting for him. He paused on the email from Simon, reading through it and then sitting back to try and digest what he had said.

Simon had written that he and Blackie were heading his way on the morrow. Arlyn squinted at the clock. That would be today, he decided, before he re-read his email. He sighed. He needed to ensure that Skylor was there. Arlyn frowned at her reaction to the pile of debris. She had shut down and hadn't responded to any of them.

Reaching for his phone, Arlyn searched his text messages, on his feet to head to the front door. Briar and Cayce were outside, a tap sounding on the door.

"What are you two doing here?" Arlyn shut the door behind them, locking it.

"To be with you." His brothers shared a look as Briar spoke. "You need us here. Why aren't you asleep?"

"Why aren't you two sleeping?" Arlyn gave a grim smile. "I'll set more coffee. We need to start compiling everything we know. Simon and Blackie are heading here today."

"They are? Then, they've found something. Where are we working? The office?" Briar headed that way, dumping the envelopes that he was holding onto the credenza. He looked around before he headed for the storeroom in the business office and returned with a roll of newsprint. He worked to tape the paper to empty spots on the wall and then hunted for coloured markers.

Cayce studied his oldest brother, a frown on his face. Arlyn looked ragged, he decided, not sure how to approach him.

"Arlyn? What can we do for you? This is hurting you. We can all see how you feel about Skylor." His hand went up as Arlyn spun to face him, his mouth opening to response, a coffee filter still held in his hand. "Don't worry. We see that because we know you so well. You have a tender heart and Skylor has claimed it."

Arlyn sighed. He had already spoken to Skylor who had just looked at him. He didn't know if she believed him or not, but it was what it was. He nodded.

"She has and I did tell her that I love her. I'm letting her find her freedom. She needs that, Cayce." Arlyn was desperate for Cayce to understand his reasoning.

"We know that too, Arlyn."

"She is finding that and in finding that freedom is finding a stronger faith. She won't say anything. Skylor's been beaten down all her life. She's now free, to some extent. I can't move in on her until she's ready. If she's ever ready." Arlyn turned back to finish setting the coffee pot to drip before he reached for the bag of muffins that his mother had given him the day before.

"She's interested, Arlyn." Cayce's words stopped Arlyn's movements. "She's interested. She just doesn't trust her emotions and instincts. She's watching you to see how you are reacting with her and to her."

Arlyn nodded, a sober look on his face. Cayce had confirmed his suspicions about Skylor. He frowned as he heard a tap at the back door and moved that way. Flipping on the outdoor light before he unlocked and opened the door, Arlyn stared in shock as Skylor stood there, a blanket wrapped around her. He reached out to draw her into the kitchen before the door was shut and locked behind her. He wrapped her into his arms, finding her tense and stiff.

"Skylor?" Arlyn waited for her to speak, knowing that it might take time for that to happen. "What happened? Why aren't you asleep?"

"I can't sleep. Where is he?" Skylor just stared at the emblem of a hawk on Arlyn's sweatshirt. She refused to look up at him.

"Where is who? Your father?" He saw her nod slightly, her face expressionless. "I don't know where he is. Do you think that he is here?"

"He is. He's found me. He'll kill me. He threatened to do that so many times." Skylor leaned against Arlyn, her eyes closing as she fought the tears that refused to not fall.

Arlyn sighed. He had expected that. He shared a look with Cayce who reached for Skylor's keys and headed down to her apartment to search it.

Cayce stared at the recording and transmission device that he found near her kitchen window. It was on the outside but it would certainly send any communication into the room. He walked back to Arlyn's home, locking the door behind him. He nodded at the look from Arlyn.

Briar had returned at that point, a frown on his face. He had no idea what had just happened but he could tell that something had. A glance at the clock let him know that it was still really early in the morning.

"Cayce? What did you find?" Arlyn shifted Skylor to a chair, crouching down beside her with an arm around her. His other hand tucked the blanket closer around her.

"A monitoring device at her kitchen window. It picks up conversation and also transmits. That has to have been set here after Joe and his crew left." Cayce was angry. He felt justified in his anger. After all, this was his brother and his lady who were being threatened.

"What?" The word exploded from Arlyn. He winced at the loudness of it. Skylor had jumped as he spoke, causing him to tighten his arm around her. "I'm sorry, Skylor. I'm so sorry. I didn't mean to frighten you."

Skylor shook her head as she turned to face Arlyn. A tear trickled down her face.

"Why me, Arlyn? What did I ever do to him? I don't understand. And I need my mother. I just don't know if she's alive or dead. He never said, just refused to speak about her." Skylor's head went down against Arlyn. She stared straight ahead as she puzzled through her thoughts.

The three brothers shared a shocked look. They had just assumed that her mother was dead. Now, with Skylor's question, they had to rethink what they had believed.

Chapter 28

Joe was angry that something had happened after he had left. He watched as the tech removed the device and bagged it. He had not expected to be called back to Arlyn's. He was due at another crime scene and had stopped here on his way past.

Arlyn stood in the kitchen doorway, watching him. He was frustrated as well. Skylor had shut down again and nothing seemed to be rousing her. He had called in his parents and his aunt. No one was able to bring her out of her withdrawal.

Joe walked towards Arlyn, pointing behind him towards the inside of the house. Arlyn backed up, almost running into Skylor who had come up behind him. He reached to wrap her into his arm, pulling her away from the door. Joe closed and locked the door. They could see the anger on his face.

"Joe?" Arlyn's voice had a question in it, the question that he was almost afraid to ask.

"It was placed sometime overnight." Joe stared at Skylor, finding her staring at the floor. "Skylor? Talk to me. Did you hear anything?"

Skylor just refused to respond. She was too afraid to. She had heard the voices, low as they were, as the men worked to place that device. She has stood in the hallway just outside of the kitchen. Skylor was sure that she would need to begin to run from there. She just didn't know where to go.

Arlyn's arm tightened on her once more. He knew that she was in flight mode. He had seen it too often with the birds that he studied. Not that she was a specimen to be studied, but the instincts to run were there. He shared a look with his brothers who each shrugged.

A quiet meow broke through the silence that covered the kitchen. The men looked around, trying to find the kitten. Arlyn began to grin as he saw Kayleigh peeking out of the blanket. The kitten continued to climb free from the blanket and then jumped to the floor. She headed for the food bowl that Arlyn kept ready for her.

"I didn't know that she had the kitten." Briar had a wide grin on her face. "Did you?"

The brothers were shaking their heads. None of them had known that. But when they stopped to think about it, it made perfect sense to them. She would not want to leave the kitten on its own, not when she was so scared.

"Skylor?" Arlyn's voice finally reached through to Skylor and she looked up at him. "Are you okay?"

Skylor shook her head. No, she decided, she was not okay and didn't know if she ever would be. She turned and walked away from the kitchen, heading for his office. She slumped onto the couch, her eyes on the paper that Briar had taped to the wall. Skylor frowned. She had no idea what the paper was for but there had to be a reason for it to be up there.

Briar had followed her, a hand laid on Arlyn's arm to stop him. Just maybe she needed to speak with someone other than Arlyn. He watched her for a moment before he sat beside her, patiently waiting for her to speak. They all knew that she would speak when she was ready and that they could not force her to.

"Briar? What's with the paper?" Skylor refused to look at him. She just sat, a sober look on her face. She was afraid and didn't know how to deal with it other than to shut down.

"The paper? We're working through what we know and what we suspect. That's our plan for today. And yes, we are setting aside our daily work just for today. You're worried about us doing that." Briar was reading her correctly, he decided.

"I see. When are you going to start doing that?" Skylor didn't see the grin that crossed Briar's face.

"Soon. I had just put the paper up when you appeared and then we found that device." Briar looked towards the hallway, seeing Arlyn standing in the shadows, his heart on his face. "And I hear that we have a couple of friends heading this way today."

Skylor shrugged. Instead of responding, she reached for a stack of papers and began to read through it, ignoring Briar as she did so.

Briar watched her for a few moments before he was on his feet, heading for Arlyn who backed away from the office. He was shaking his head as he approached his brother.

"She's not communicating her feelings, Arlyn. How do we get her to do that?"

"I know. We just have to wait. Something will trigger her emotions to break and when they do, it will be a wild ride for her. I'm glad that Eavan and Julia are heading this way today as well. She needs to hear their stories again and again." Arlyn rubbed at his cheek. He had no idea how to help his lady or even how to solve what they were going through. He had no idea if he was bringing danger to her or if she was bringing it to him. There was just not enough information to determine that.

"That's what I'm afraid of. We've given her all the verses that we can. We've prayed for her and with her. Aunt Anna and Mom are trying to reach through to her but they both said it's difficult to do that."

"It is. She's had so many years of being held captive and being beaten down. It will take time and a lot of counselling for her to get through this." Briar gave a brief smile at his brother. "And you need to be there for her, Arlyn. You're her lifeline in all of this. And if you disappear or are hurt, it will devastate her and drive her even deeper into the darkness."

"I know, Briar. I know. There is just no way that we can prevent either one of those events from happening. I just wish this was over. I want whoever it is. But I have to let God be the Avenger. Vengeance is His. I realize that, Briar. It doesn't change how I feel though."

"It is His to avenge. We know that." Briar shared a look with Cayce who now stood behind his brother. "Where's Joe?"

"He's gone." Cayce shoved gently at Ashlyn's shoulder. "Go and be with your lady, Arlyn. She needs you."

"I know." Arlyn rubbed at the back of his neck before he walked into the office and then sat beside Skylor. He clasped his hands together without looking at her. He prayed for the words that he needed and didn't have them.

Skylor jumped as she felt the couch sink beside her. She shot a sidelong glance to her right and sighed. Of course, Arlyn would be there. He wanted to solve all of her problems for her, including who was after her, and he couldn't. She waited for him to hug her and when he didn't, she just leaned against him, hearing his prayer for her.

———

Chapter 29

Simon and Blackie walked towards Arlyn where he stood outside of his house. Their wives were with them. Arlyn had a grim look on his face, causing the two men to frown at him.

"Simon? Blackie? You're here. I'm not sure that I like this." He shook their hands and then hugged the ladies. "Skylor's in the office with Briar and Cayce, ladies." He turned and walked in with them, leaving Simon and Blackie to follow. "Skylor? Do you have a moment?" Arlyn waited patiently for her to respond. When she turned, he reached out a hand, again waiting for her to take it. When she did, Arlyn tugged her towards him. "This is Julia, Blackie's wife, you remember. And this is Eavan, Simon's wife. Her name is unusual. Her adoptive parents were Irish and chose that for her. It's pronounced E-veen."

Skylor studied the ladies in silence. It was disconcerting to be studied in that way unless one had been warned about that. Both the ladies were prepared for that. Skylor finally reached to hug them, surprising everyone with her actions. She surprised herself as well.

"Thank you for coming." Skylor felt a sense of panic rising within her. She was not good in social situations, not yet anyway. "What do you have for us?"

Julia grinned at her, an arm around her to turn her to face the wall. She then walked the two of them along the walls, reading what had been notated there.

"You've been busy. I like that. Now, where do we begin?" Julia shared a look with Blackie, who was nodding.

"We do have information for you, Skylor." Blackie's voice behind her had her jumping in fear. He sighed as she spun to stare at him, her face white with her fear and her eyes huge. "It's okay to be afraid, Skylor. You are thrust into something that you didn't want or don't understand. And you don't have the understanding of life that the rest of us do in order to properly assess the threat facing you."

Skylor was nodding, relieved that finally someone understood her and could vocalize her feelings and thoughts.

"Thank you, Blackie. You have put into words what I am feeling." Skylor looked around in panic, not seeing Arlyn for a moment. She drew in a deep breath, ready to walk away and find until. Arlyn suddenly appeared beside her and wrapped her into a hug. "Arlyn?"

"Let's sit for a bit, love. We need to spend some time in prayer for both of us." He gently shoved her to a seat on the couch and sat beside her, an arm around her. He watched her closely, seeing her struggling to escape the chains that held her captive.

Simon started off their time of prayer, quickly followed by the others. Ardan concluded their time of prayer. No one raised their heads very quickly, feeling the presence of God in the room.

Blackie shared a look with Julia before she nodded.

"Skylor? You've heard our story. Now, you need to hear Eavan's. We have not been in each other's lives for many years, separated by our mother when she abandoned Eavan as a newborn. Eavan has had to deal with that. She was raised by a wonderful couple and has her Grandmother still in her life." Julia motioned to Eavan.

Eavan began to speak, Simon's arm around her, as she told her story. She then mentioned the stories of a friend of theirs, Leah, who had been raised in a rough household as well. Skylor sank closer to Arlyn, finally realizing that her situation, while it had gone on for a long time, was something that happened to others. Her sobs began to fill the room as the chains tying her to her past were finally broken. Arlyn's arms just held his lady, his heart breaking for her.

The others in the room looked on with sympathy and then turned to the multitude of papers that lay on the desk. Briar had made enough copies for everyone, including Joe. Conversation was quiet, with their eyes turning every once in a while to Skylor.

Skylor's sobs finally slowed and then stopped. She took the warm damp cloth that Anna handed her and swiped at her face. Skylor then realized that Arlyn was holding her tightly. She looked up at him, a puzzled look on her face as he simply smiled at her.

"All done with the water works?" He dropped a kiss on her cheek. "How be we see what the others have come up with?"

Skylor nodded, rising to her feet reluctantly and walking around the room to read what had been placed on the paper. She was surprised to see how much information there really was there. Simon had been watching her and rose to walk beside her, waiting for her to speak.

"Simon? What is all this?" Skylor gestured at the paper.

"This is what we have discovered. I have spoken to another friend and she has passed on what information she has been able to find and it has been a lot."

"I see." Skylor blinked. "I am going to owe everyone so much money." She looked up as she heard a sound from Simon. "Simon?"

"We never charge friends. Even the friend I approached will never charge you. It's how we are the hands and feet of God on earth." Simon smiled at her. "What questions do you have?"

"Questions? You want questions from me? I have even thought of that yet." Skylor walked away to read once more the information. They could all see that she was struggling to understand what she was reading.

Arlyn stopped beside his father, finding his father laying an arm across his shoulders. Ardan prayed for his son and then for Skylor. They could all see that something had changed with Skylor, that something had reached deep into her and given her freedom. They just didn't know what had done that.

"She's breaking free of whatever it has been that has held her captive. I'm glad, Dad. I just don't know where it leaves us." Arlyn turned and walked away, his shoulders slumping. He wasn't there to hear the exclamation from Skylor or to see how she turned to find him, her face dropping as she realized that he wasn't there.

Chapter 30

Looking up from where he had been standing and leaning on the kitchen counter, Arlyn turned as he found Skylor almost running at him. His arms opened as she approached. He was glad that he was leaning against something. He was convinced afterwards that they would have landed on the floor by the force with which she hit him. His arms simply wrapped around her and held her.

"Skylor? What happened? What did you find out?" Arlyn spoke at last, his face leaning against her head.

"I found out that the man is not my father. I have no idea who he is or where my parents are. He kidnapped me when I was a year old. Is that why he kept me hidden away?" Skylor's body was shaking from the force of her emotions.

"He's not? Who told you that?" Arlyn's eyes found those of his mother who had followed Skylor, highly worried about the younger lady.

"Simon. That was the information that they had found. He said someone else had found that information and passed it on to him." Skylor felt Arlyn nodding. "Who are my parents? And where are they? And why?"

"I don't know, love, but we'll figure it out. He's come up with names?"

"He has. He had a copy of my birth certificate. My name is the same. At least, he didn't change that.

———

I just want to know why. And I want to meet my parents." Skylor drew in a shaky sob. "It's not fair, Arlyn. It's not fair that he stole my life from me."

Arlyn nodded once more. He knew that she was really hurting and that he would need to find someone to speak with her. He just didn't know who. Perhaps Simon or Blackie would know of someone.

"How be we go back in there and see what you found." Arlyn turned her back towards the office, nodding at his mother as she moved past him into the kitchen. He knew that she would be making coffee and tea and finding snacks for them.

"Okay. But how does that go with what you've gone through? Are they involved in the black market?" Skylor was hardly able to make sense with her words, feeling as if she was talking as a child.

"I don't know, love, but we'll figure it out. Between us and Joe, we'll do that." Arlyn walked towards the first paper, reading what information had been added. He walked Skylor along the wall, reading each paper. He could hear the hum of conversation around him, with the odd laugh interspersed among the words. Arlyn frowned at the new information. He would need to digest it, he knew, and that would take time.

Simon and Blackie were waiting for them as they finished reading the last paper. The two men were highly worried about the couple, knowing that they were not done with this adventure or whatever it was called. They both knew what it was like to be at this point in that said adventure.

<hr>

153

"Simon? Blackie? What else can you tell us?" Arlyn kept an arm around his lady, keeping her tight to his side.

"What you see on the walls? That's a summary of what we have found. We're still working on it. Dad has headed for Skylor's home town to see what he can discover." Blackie was worried about his father, knowing that this was a dangerous yet necessary move. "He'll be there a couple of days, he thinks."

"He can't do that!" Skylor's voice was hoarse, given how much that she had wept that day.

"He already has, Skylor." Blackie walked away at that, his emotions raw for a moment. Julie reached to hug him, her eyes on Skylor.

Skylor struggled to walk away from Arlyn. He finally released her, to watch her walk from the room. Cayce quietly followed her, seeing that she was heading out of the house and to her apartment. He sighed. They needed to let her have space to grieve what she had lost but he was highly worried about her. He walked back up to the office, not sure what to say.

Arlyn looked up from his computer hours later. He was alone in his house, alone that was except for Skylor. She had returned not that long ago, determined to make sense of what was going on. He didn't think that they had enough information to do that but he was willing to work with her. Arlyn had been working away on his own tasks, looking up once in a while to see Skylor staring at the paper that lined the walls.

He rose, heading for her and just sitting beside her. He began to pray audibly for her, finding her leaning against him. Arlyn begged God for his lady's safety and then begged for protection for her. He didn't pay for himself. He didn't think to do that.

"Where is God, Arlyn?" Skylor was struggling with her faith, knowing in her heart that God was in control, loved her, and only wanted the best for her. In her mind, she didn't believe that anyone, even God, could love her.

"He's right here, Skylor. He's right here. He's walked this path before us and is walking it with us right now. He knows what we face. God is our Protector and will hide us in the cleft of the rock and cover us there. He is using us to bring someone to justice. He will also use what you have gone through to bring a blessing to others." Arlyn frowned, a thought crossing his mind. "Skylor? Did you finish high school?"

"I did. It was done on line, something that he set up with a school out of the area. I didn't have any choice. My contact with that school had to go through him." Skylor sighed, a wistful look on her face. "I wanted to go to college but I wasn't allowed to. Do you know how that beats you down?"

"No, I can't say that I do. I can't totally understand how your life played out. You can still go to college." Arlyn reached to give her a hug.

"Oh, I'm not smart enough to do that." Skylor was parroting the words that had been spewed at her many times a day.

"But you see, you are. You're an intelligent, beautiful lady who I am happy to call my friend. You are loved by my family and my friends. You can do what you want with your life. We will support you in your decisions."

Skylor had turned her face to look up at him, seeing that look in his eyes again. She sighed.

"I guess. What would I ever study?" Skylor had thought many times of what she wanted to study but knew that it was fruitless to even decide.

"You don't have to make a decision in the next weeks or months. You need to heal and that will take time. College courses can be taken on line or you can go in person. Pray over it. We'll pray with you." Arlyn settled back against the couch before he glanced at his watch. "It's suppertime, Skylor. Let's go out for a meal."

"Go out? We can't. It's not safe." Skylor protested even though hope shone in her eyes. The breakthrough that she had experienced earlier that day was giving her a reason to believe that her life could change. God was working in her heart and she could only thank God that Arlyn was in her life. She didn't realize that she had fallen in love with this tall, handsome man.

"We're not hiding, Skylor. Not any more. If we continue to hide, this will never be over. We pray over what we want to do and then we move forward." Arlyn bit at his lip, wanting to say something but not sure how to proceed.

Skylor tilted her head to study him. She frowned for a moment before she spoke.

"Arlyn? You wanted to say something?"

"I do. Just listen for a moment. I don't want you to make a decision right away. I told you that I love you. I want to marry you, Skylor, to be the one who protects you and loves you and walks beside you through life. I don't know if or when you'll be ready to accept that. Pray over it. Talk to Mom or Aunt Anna or one of our friends. They'll give you the counsel that you need." Arlyn dropped a kiss on her cheek, seeing the look of wonder and hope on her face. He reached to draw her to her feet, walking them out of the house, and then to his truck before he drove away to find that restaurant that he wanted to take her to.

Chapter 31

Skylor froze in place the next morning as she saw the man walking towards her, an evil grin on his face. Her father, as she still thought of him, had found her and she was deeply afraid. She backed away before she turned and ran, heading for somewhere she could hide. She gave a scream as two men appeared beside her and grabbed at her hands, pulling her with them.

The two men were undercover officers, sent to watch Skylor. They tugged her into an abandoned building and then through it before heading for a vehicle. Shouts sounded behind them but the words were muffled.

Skylor shook with fear, not understanding that she was safe. She struggled to escape, not able to release her wrist from the grip of the younger man. Finally, his words reached through to her and she stopped her motions, staring at him.

"You're helping me?" Skylor had not expected that. No one had done that in her past.

"We are. Joe asked us to watch out for you." Will turned and looked behind him. "Who was that?"

"The man I thought was my father." Skylor drew in a deep breath, finding that she no longer feared him. "I'm not afraid of him. Not any more."

"No? That's good but you still need to be very cautious, Skylor." Will's head was in constant motion, looking for anyone who might mean Skylor harm.

"We're going to take you to meet with Joe. He needs to know what just happened."

"Of course he does." Skylor sighed. "And so will Arlyn. Only he's out in the forest somewhere for the day. I finished what I needed to do in the office and just had to get out of there. I never had the freedom to choose what I wanted to do before. Not until now. And this happens."

Will gave a brief grin at her grumblings. He didn't fully understand what she had been through but he did know that she was in danger. He and his partner, Bob, would do everything that they could to protect her and prevent her from disappearing. That was the rumour on the street, that she was to disappear. And that meant that she would die. They knew the Koyle brothers from school and wanted to prevent any harm coming to one of their ladies.

Joe watched Skylor from where he stood in his office doorway. She was walking towards him, flanked by Will and Bob. He sighed. Something had to happen for them to be here.

"Skylor?" Joe's voice brought her eyes to him. He could see the anger in her and nodded. She was breaking free of the bonds that had held her for so many years. He was glad to see it happen but it also made it much more dangerous for her. She was apt to walk into danger without realizing it.

"Joe? What is going on? That man showed up and tried to abduct me. Where am I safe?" Skylor almost stomped by him and headed into his office.

Joe grinned at Will and Bob before he nodded towards his office. The two men followed him, watching Skylor's reaction. They were not sure what to expect from her. They were not used to protecting someone like her.

"Skylor? What happened? Why were you out on your own?"

"I needed to do that, Joe. I can't hide any more. And Arlyn is away for his work. He can't be with me all the time. I don't want that. I can't be smothered." Skylor dared Joe to contradict her.

Joe merely stared back at her, his thoughts tumbling over themselves. He was well aware that Skylor was rebelling and decided that it was about time. Only it wasn't the right time to be rebelling.

"We'll get you home, Skylor. For now, you need to stay here." Joe walked away with the two officers, deep in conversation. He didn't see Skylor peeking out of his office and then walking rapidly from the building, heading for home. Returning to his office, Joe came to a sudden halt before he spun and headed for the desk officer. "Where's Skylor?"

The officer looked around, surprised at the question.

"Isn't she with you?"

"No, she's not." Joe's eyes slid closed. She had taken off again and he had no idea where she was. And he couldn't leave the building. He had interviews waiting to happen. "Can you send a patrol officer to her home?"

Skylor hid in her apartment. She had felt that she had been followed and had almost ran for her home. She had not realized that it would be that long a walk, not realizing that her fear made it seem that much longer. Reaching for a blanket, Skylor wrapped it around herself and then found her spot on the couch. Her eyes closed as tears trickled down her face. She was deeply afraid, more afraid than she had ever been. Skylor didn't realize that this was a natural consequence of her freedom from her captor. And captor he had been.

Arlyn parked in his normal spot on the driveway, slumping slightly for a moment before he climbed down from the truck and reached for the samples he had collected that day and then for the bag containing his camera. Once in his office, he dropped what he was holding onto the work table and then stepped back. It was almost dark. His work had taken him longer than he had planned. Over the day, Arlyn had felt someone watching him but had not seen anyone. That worried him.

Walking through his house, Arlyn paused. Something felt off and he had no idea what it was. He shrugged, thinking that it was the weight of the trouble and danger that he felt. He showered and changed to his night clothes. Reaching for his phone, he sent off a text to Skylor and then watched for a response. None came and that troubled him. Arlyn sighed before he sat on the side of his bed, praying for his lady, before he crawled under the covers. He was exhausted and was asleep almost as soon as his head hit his pillow.

Two hours later, Skylor reached for her phone, reading through her messages. She had been asleep when Arlyn had returned home and missed his text message. She gave a sad smile. Skylor was trying to make up her mind about what to do and how to protect Arlyn. She thought that running might be the only way to do that. Only, Arlyn would never let her do that. Not if he knew what she was planning. Of that she was certain. Skylor jumped as she heard scrapes at the door and then at the windows, a hand covering her mouth to cover her scream. Someone was out there. She was too terrified to reach for her phone once more and call for help. Skylor had never had that certainty and comfort that someone would help her. She was still living under the threats from the man who called himself her father and those would continue to restrain her for now.

Finally, Skylor rose to her feet and cautiously crept to look out of the windows in the door and then moved from window to window, carefully drawing the drapes to one side only enough to peek out. She didn't see anyone but she felt the threat out there. She didn't know what to do about it. She needed to talk with Arlyn and he was not available.

Skylor crept to her bed, to lie awake over the night. She shivered with her fear, not sure what was causing it other than what she had been through. She didn't think that God was there, not feeling the touch on her hand. An angel stood watch over her that night, sent by God for her protection. She finally slept in the early morning hours, not hearing the taps and scrapes that once more sounded around her apartment. She also didn't hear the noise that came from Arlyn's place as the door was broken in and Arlyn was dragged from his bed, forced to dress into casual clothes, and then dragged from the house.

The front door swung open in the wind that had risen. The wind swept through the entry way, disturbing anything that was in its way. The wind died down as dawn broke out in the eastern sky.

Three hours later, Bessie paused at the doorway, fear on her face as she stepped inside, calling for her son. She searched for him and didn't find him. She walked back outside and made the call that she dreaded to make. Arlyn had disappeared and she couldn't find him. Only the police would be able to do that.

Chapter 32

Bessie watched from the sidewalk as the officers moved into Arlyn's home, worry about her son almost more than she could handle. She spied Skylor opening her apartment door and then being walked over to where Bessie was waiting. Bessie wrapped an arm around Skylor, not sure what to say.

"Bessie? What's going on? Where's Arlyn?" Skylor looked around, still not quite fully awake, and not seeing him.

"He's not there, Skylor. He's gone." Bessie drew in a breath that was more a sob. She had reached out to Ardan and the boys. They were away for the day at a conference and hadn't responded to her text messages.

"He's gone? When? Oh! I didn't hear anything. I mean. I heard something late last night but then I slept. Oh, I shouldn't have slept. Maybe I would have heard them." Skylor was working herself into a fine state at the thought that she might have prevented this.

"I don't know that you would have been able to stop anything. In fact, you might well have disappeared as well." Bessie turned as Anna appeared at her side. "Anna?"

"Arlyn?" At Bessie's nod, Anna's face tightened. "I was afraid of this. Who's investigating? Joe's away today."

"I have no idea." Bessie moved Skylor to lean against her car. "I have no idea." She was repeating her words, not aware that she was. She was just that worried about her son and then for her son's lady.

Skylor slumped against the car, watching the activity around the house. She sighed. She had done this, she decided. She had brought trouble to Arlyn. Skylor didn't take into account that Arlyn was already a target and she was collateral damage to that.

Cayce and Briar appeared at her apartment door late that afternoon. She stepped back to let them in, accepting their hugs as they passed her. She stood for a moment, staring out of the open door before she quietly closed it. Skylor turned to watch the brothers, seeing the emotions that they were trying hard to hide.

"Cayce? Briar? Weren't you at an all-day conference?" Skylor headed for her office where she had been trying to make sense of everything.

"We were, but you are more important than that." Cayce moved after her as Briar headed for the kitchen, searching for anything that he could find for them to eat. Briar doubted that Skylor had eaten that day.

"No, I'm not." Skylor's steps stopped as Cayce's hand found her wrist. "I'm not, Cayce. I really am not."

"But you see, you are, Skylor. You are important enough that God sent His Son to die to pay the debt you owed. You are that precious to Him." Cayce was desperate to get Skylor to understand that.

Skylor thought through what Cayce had said and finally nodded. She understood at last what they had all been saying to her. She had been beaten down so much in her spirit that it took time and many reinforcements of that fact.

"I finally understand, Cayce." Her voice was barely above a whisper. Tears momentarily blinded her. "I finally get it. That man beat me down so far that I don't know who I am any more."

Cayce hugged her, knowing that she would be a sister to him if Arlyn had his wish fulfilled.

"I'm glad, Skylor. We're praying for you and will continue to do that. You are precious to us all, but particularly Arlyn. He's in love with you but won't move ahead with that while you're healing." Cayce frowned as she gave a small smile. "Skylor?" He heard Briar coming to a stop behind him.

"He's told me that, Cayce. And that has helped. He makes me feel as if I'm special to someone. You don't understand how that matters to me. I have never felt special to anyone." Skylor turned away as she finished speaking, not seeing the brothers trying to control their emotions.

"What have you discovered?" Briar set down the tray that he was holding and headed for her desk. He reached for one of the stacks of paper that she had tidily set on the desktop.

"I'm not sure. I was looking on the internet for my name and found information that I don't understand. I also looked for my parents and found that." She pointed at the stack that he was holding. "And Simon, Blackie, and Samuel had sent on information that I don't understand. Can you help me?

And will it find Arlyn and bring him home?" Skylor was very worried about him, needing him with her in order to feel stable and safe.

Cayce reached for another stack, reading through it and making notes. Briar was doing the same. Skylor was deep in reading what Samuel had sent her. She didn't understand it all and then drew up the email and started to respond. She wasn't sure if she was doing it correctly. Briar looked at her for a moment and then reached to help her. She glanced at him with a small smile before her concentration went back to what she was typing. Skylor sighed. She wasn't writing very fast with just two fingers but it was what it was.

Anna found them an hour later, Bessie and Ardan beside her. They reached for piles of paper as well before Cayce headed to Arlyn's home and returned with the papers from the wall. He and Briar worked to tape them to the walls and then continued to add information as it was found.

Skylor looked up at some point, a frown on her face as she stared into the distance. She was troubled by what she was reading and struggling to understand it. Her phone chiming had her searching for it and then answering it.

"Skylor? It's Blackie. How are you?" Blackie had been burdened for her. "Any word on Arlyn?"

"Not a word. And I'm scared for him. Blackie? How do we find out if there really is black market for those birds?" Skylor's voice sounded loud in the sudden silence in the room. "I mean. He could have disappeared because of me but what if it isn't?"

"That's our thought, Skylor. I have reached out to that friend again. Emma has found a wealth on information that she has forwarded to me and also to Joe. Are you around tomorrow?" Blackie grinned as he heard her snort.

"Of course, I am. Where else would I be?" Skylor grew quiet, not sure how to express herself. "Blackie? If it were you, what would you do? How would you go about what we need to prove?"

Blackie nodded to himself. Skylor was growing in her personality and in what she wanted. Her captivity bonds had been broken and she was reaching out for help, something that she had never been able to do.

"I'll think about it, Skylor. When we meet tomorrow, I will go over my thoughts with you. For now, I would try and stay safe and stay around people who love me and care about me. Is Arlyn's family with you?" He grinned as he heard her disgruntled "yes". "That's good, Skylor. They will do what they can to protect you and help you through this. You are not alone. Never again will you be alone. That's is a guarantee that each one of us will work to keep."

Skylor set her phone aside, rubbing at her eyes. She looked around at the people in her home and smiled. She was welcomed by them and had become part of their family.

Chapter 33

Two days later, Skylor rose from her desk. She didn't think that she had left it much over the past few days. She thought that she was beginning to finally understand what had happened to her but she still had doubts.

Blackie and Simon had been around the day before, bringing more information that had confused her. They had tried their best to explain everything to her, including what they had discovered about her true family.

Skylor was confused about her true family. She didn't have enough information, she decided, to understand that. But there was a light in the distance for her. She just needed the right person to explain it all for her.

Walking outside and around the yards, Skylor was sad and sober. She missed Arlyn and prayed for him, for his protection, and for his swift return to home. She had been in the business office, trying to understand what needed to be done. Skylor had studied the photos on the walls and then the stuffed birds, a finger coming out to touch one of them. Arlyn had told her that Briar had done the taxidermy work on them.

Back in her house, Skylor reached for a bottle of juice. She should eat but didn't feel hungry. Hearing a tap at her door, she spun, fear momentarily moving through her. She crept to the door, finding Simon standing there with a couple who she didn't recognize.

"Skylor? May we come in?" Simon grinned at her.

Skylor frowned at him and then at the couple with him.

"Weren't you just here yesterday? Now what did you find?" Skylor stepped back to let the trio enter. "Who is with you?"

Simon grinned at her again. She was getting feisty, he decided, and he was glad to see that. She still would retreat into her silence, which was to be expected given what she had been through all of her life.

"This is Abe and Emma Finlay. They're the friends Blackie mentioned. Abe has a security team and Emma has a business to track people and events and whatever needs to be found. She has information that she needs to go over with you." Simon looked around. "Do we meet in your office?"

Skylor shrugged. Simon headed that way as she hesitated. Abe followed him as Emma waited for Skylor.

"Skylor? May I call you that?" Emma waited for Skylor to nod. "You're afraid and trying hard to hide it. I've been there. Abe and I had a ten-year long adventure that we'll share with you. For now, let me pray with you. That is the only thing that got me through." Emma did that, waiting for Skylor to nod in agreement. "And it's okay to cry, scream, vent, get mad, yell, direct it at God and then repent and ask for forgiveness. He knows we're human and will react as a human will. I've done all that. I approach God as our Abba Father."

"I don't have that, you know. I never have had. All I had was a man who abused me to the point that I shut down for far too long."

"I understand that, Skylor. I understand that you have spoken on the phone with Rachel and Gideon. They are friends of ours. They both had an abusive foster family. In fact, their foster father killed his biological daughter to keep his wife in line. That should not have happened."

Skylor didn't take her eyes from Emma. She could see Abe and Simon behind Emma. She was not certain to know what to say.

"That is so sad, Emma. It could have been me. I think that's what he wants, to kill me. But I don't understand how I ended up here or how Arlyn is involved in all this." Skylor was sober as she spoke before she brushed by Emma and headed for her office.

Abe and Emma shared a look. It was about how she was expected to react and they had prepared themselves for it.

Late that afternoon, Skylor locked the door behind the trio, her forehead resting against the wood. She was exhausted and sore in spirit and soul. She was also overwhelmed by the wealth of material that the trio had left them. Skylor could not comprehend it all at that point. She needed to walk away from it and go back to it the next day.

―――

Skylor's thoughts returned to the present, her thoughts still troubled. She missed Arlyn greatly, worried about what he was facing and if he would return alive or dead. She was saddened at that last thought but was enough of a realist to know that it was a real possibility.

Reaching for her phone, Skylor scrolled through her messages. A smile lit her face at the comments from the brothers and then softened as she read the parent messages from Ardan and Bessie and the aunt messages from Anna. Skylor frowned at the messages from Joe, knowing that she would need to speak with him on the next day.

She set aside her phone, silence in the apartment. It was a different silence from what she had been used to. It was a silence that spoke of love and welcoming and safety. Skylor headed for her bedroom, dropping to the bed and then sleeping. She didn't rouse for the whole night, the sleep deep and restorative.

On her feet the next morning just as dawn was breaking, Skylor headed for her office. There was something there that drew her, something that had been said the day before. She searched through the paperwork until she found the page that she wanted. Skylor read it over and over, finally setting it aside. She had no idea where Emma found that information, but she had and now Skylor had to deal with it. It saddened her to realize that she not likely would ever meet her parents, not on earth. Emma had uncovered their death certificates. That lady had been really sorry to hand them over, having a suspicion that Skylor had hopes that her parents were still alive.

Joe took the papers that were handed to him, his eyes on Skylor. He frowned. There was something different about her that day and he wasn't sure what it was. He read through the paperwork, knowing that he likely had a copy in his email inbox. He would deal with it later. For now, he read back over the results of Emma's investigation.

"They're dead, aren't they, Joe? I'll never get to meet them." Skylor was sober as she spoke, her emotions tamped down as far as she could do that.

"It looks like it. Emma would not have stated that unless she was sure. It's what she does. She never presents anything unless it has been proven and proven in more than one way. She also finds information that no one else seems to be able to find."

"I get that. I just wish that it was different. Abe gave me some information and tips on how to stay safe. It might work but then again it might not. I'm not hiding any more, Joe. I'm going to be out and about. That may draw whoever these people are out."

Joe had listened carefully to her words. He fully expected her to do that. He also had a list of names of volunteers to be with her.

Chapter 34

Skylor once more walked through the down town of Grasspoint. She was afraid but determined not to show it. She knew that Will and Bob were flanking her, seeming to be just other pedestrians. They had nodded at her as she had approached them.

Looking up at the names of the stores, Skylor reached for the door to one of them. She entered a little tea shop, having always wanted to eat in one. She looked around and then found a seat by herself. Will and Bob had entered as well and found seats near her.

When she was almost done her meal, Skylor looked up in surprise and then fear as a man pulled out a chair and sat down across from her. She shrank back against her chair as she faced the man who had been her abuser.

"So, I finally find you on your own." He sneered at her, frowning as well as he didn't see the fear that was usually on her face. "You're coming with me."

Skylor watched as Will and Bob rose to their feet and approached to stand behind him. She drew in a deep breath, knowing that she was facing her enemy and would come forth victorious from it.

"No, I don't think so. You have no right or reason for me to go with you. You have done enough to ruin my life." Skylor's voice stayed even. She was terrified of the man and what he could do but she was not going with him. That she had determined in herself not to do.

"Oh, but you are. Now, on your feet!" Jed Smith looked up at her with anger on his face. She had escaped from him and that would not happen again. He shoved back his chair and rose, his hands reaching for her as anger coloured his face. Only, his hands never reached her. His arms were caught in the hands of Will and Bob. Smith struggled to escape and was unable to escape the hands of two strong young police officers.

Briar and Cayce had entered the shop, intent on enjoying a late morning tea. They stared in shock at the scene in front of them before they moved to stand on either side of Skylor's chair. Their hands rested on her shoulders as they struggled to understand what was going on.

Skylor jumped as she felt their hands and glanced up quickly. She sighed to herself. Of course, they would show up, just to stand in the gap for Arlyn. Her attention went back to Smith, seeing him struggling to get to her despite the handcuffs.

Will tucked his phone away. He had reached out to Joe, who had been shocked at the gall of Smith to appear in broad daylight and try to kidnap Skylor. He was on his feet and running for the tea room, sliding to a stop at the door and then shooting through it. He took in the scene, seeing the anger and fear that Skylor was trying had to hide. Joe knew that she had had years of suppressing her emotions. They were all over the place now, he knew, and that was not going to help keep her safe.

Smith was shoved out of the tea room and into the hands of patrol officers who in turn shoved him into a patrol vehicle and then shoved into a cell at the police department. He had been booked and would now be questioned. Joe had reached out to another investigator to do that.

Joe turned to face Skylor and then shared a look with the two brothers. He sighed to himself as he slid back a chair and then waited for Skylor to speak. When she didn't, he sighed once more.

"Skylor? What did you go and do?" Joe waited for her to speak, seeing the anger sparking from her eyes.

"I did nothing. All I did was come in here for tea. He appeared." Skylor frowned at Joe. "He had to be following me or had someone following me."

"He likely did. We'll find out for sure when we interrogate him." Joe looked up at the two men standing beside Skylor. "You need to go home, Skylor, at least for now. Let Briar and Cayce take you there. I'll be in touch with you." Joe strode from the room, leaving Skylor staring after him, her mouth opening and closing as if she wanted to protest.

"Come on, Skylor. Joe's right. You need to get home." Briar waited for Skylor to rise. Cayce had disappeared to find his truck and bring it back to stop right outside of the tea room.

Skylor struggled with her emotions as she stood, Briar's hand out to catch her elbow and guide her from the room. His hand raised to wave at the tea room owner. He would be back, he knew, to take care of Skylor's meal.

———

Tucked into the truck, Skylor stared out of the windows, her thoughts troubled. Smith had been arrested and that began a new era in her life. She wasn't sure that she was ready for that, but God had led her so far in this and in bringing in friends who were helping her to heal. Skylor knew that it would take time. The only person who she really wanted to see was Arlyn, and he wasn't there.

Walking through her apartment late that afternoon, Skylor was sober and distraught. Joe had called her, just to let her know that Smith was not speaking, refusing to speak in fact. That disturbed her. Smith had a lot to answer for. He just didn't want to give any answers.

Skylor's head tilted as she heard subtle sounds from Arlyn's home. They were the sounds of footsteps and sounded familiar. She reached for her keys and cautiously left her apartment to walk up to the back door. Her hand reached for the door knob which twisted under her hand and the door creaked open. Skylor drew in a deep breath, looking around as she entered.

Hearing sounds from down the hall, Skylor stood just outside of the kitchen doorway, frowning as she heard the sound of running water and then the opening and closing of a door. It was strange, she decided, and reached for her phone. She sighed. She had left it on her kitchen table.

A hand covered her mouth as Skylor heard footsteps heading through the bedroom and towards the hallway. She knew those footsteps. Arlyn was home. And she didn't understand how that was possible.

Arlyn's steps paused as he neared the bedroom doorway. He sensed that someone else was in the house but that person didn't mean him any harm. He walked slowly forward, staring down the hallway before his face softened and he moved rapidly towards Skylor. Skylor hesitated for only a second and then flew towards him to be wrapped tightly in his arms. They both wept, their sobs heavy at time. Skylor finally leaned back to look up at him, seeing the ravages of what he had been through but seeing his love for her shining in his eyes.

"Marry me, Skylor. Please marry me?" Arlyn's head went back down on his beloved's head as he just stood and held her. It was as if he was dreaming but he knew that this was reality.

Chapter 35

Skylor turned from where she had been preparing a meal for Arlyn. He had sat at his table, his head in his hands. He was exhausted and knew that he needed to see a physician and also to speak with Joe. He had simply sent Joe a text message that he was home but could Joe give him the night? Joe had responded quickly, simply with a "yes" and then the question of whether Arlyn was okay.

"Arlyn? What happened?" Skylor slid the plate with scrambled eggs and toast in front of Arlyn, before she set her own plate down. She reached for their coffees before she was in a seat beside him.

"I can't talk right now, Skylor. I need to speak with Joe." He sighed as he heard the door bell. He didn't want to speak with anyone but it looked as if that was not to happen.

Joe stood in the doorway, a stern look on his face. He had not felt comfortable leaving his talk with Arlyn until the next day. There had been information received just in the last hour that Arlyn now had a hit out on him and that needed to be addressed.

Dropping his laptop on the kitchen table, Joe reached for a mug of coffee and then sat, taking with thanks the food that Skylor set in front of him. He studied her, seeing the subtle changes in her that spoke of what she was going through and how she was dealing with it all.

"Joe?" Arlyn looked up and sighed. "You want to talk."

"I do. Eat your meal and then we pray. You're in deep danger, Arlyn, and we can't get a handle on why." Joe watched as Skylor rose and headed for the business office to return with a file folder that she handed him. "What is this?"

"I just found that today. I have no idea how long it's been sitting in the office. For months, I would suspect. Arlyn has not been concentrating on his paperwork and this was at the bottom of the pile." Skylor sat again. She studied her plate and then shoved it to one side. She no longer had an appetite.

Joe finally reached for his laptop, his eyes on Arlyn. He needed Arlyn to talk to him. He just wasn't sure if he would. Skylor was not leaving Arlyn's side, he could tell. Joe would work with that.

"Arlyn? Talk to me. What happened? And how did you end up back here?" Joe's fingers were poised over the keyboard of his laptop, even though he had set the video program to record Arlyn's statement.

"What happened?" Arlyn rubbed at his face. "I'm not sure what actually happened, Joe. I'm really not sure." Arlyn bowed his head for a moment. He was exhausted and sore and worried. He didn't know how to deal with anything any more. He wasn't even able to pray coherently at the moment but he knew that God heard the words of his heart.

Arlyn's thoughts drifted back to that night when he had been pulled from a deep sleep and from his bed and forced to dress. He felt the hands on his shoulders once more as he was shoved from his home and into a truck. He also felt again the handcuffs that had clicked around his wrists.

Driven away from his home, Arlyn frantically twisted in his seat to study where he was being taken. It was too dark to really know where he was heading in the truck. The men were silent before one of them dropped a blindfold over his eyes. Arlyn had struggled even more to escape to no avail.

Arlyn was shoved from the truck hard enough so that he landed on his hands and knees. He drew in a deep breath as pain shot through his body. Hauled to his feet, Arlyn stumbled as he was forced to walk along a gravel path, stumbling as he did so. He had trouble staying upright, only the rough grip on his upper arm holding him in that position.

Hearing the rough creak of a rusty door hinge, Arlyn drew in a deep breath. He had no chance to try and escape before he was shoved into a room and the handcuffs removed. A rough voice ordered him not to remove the blindfold or he would pay the price.

Waiting for what seemed to be forever, Arlyn reached to remove the cloth that blocked his vision. He rubbed at his eyes for a moment before he opened them and stared around. He rubbed at his wrists, still feeling the cold steel of the handcuffs that had shackled him. On his feet, Arlyn began a systematic search of the shed or outbuilding or whatever it was that he was locked into.

He couldn't find a way out and that frustrated him. He searched once more for anything that he could use as a weapon and again found nothing. Arlyn stared at the rough bunk that sat against one wall and then pulled back a shower curtain that hid a toilet and stained sink. He frowned and then sighed. He had no way out. There were windows but they were nailed shut.

Arlyn sank down onto the bunk, a hand rubbing at his face. He had no idea who the men were or what they wanted. He bowed his head, defeat uppermost in his mind. He had tried to stay upbeat but the burden had bowed him and almost broken him. Arlyn sat that way for what was hours before he was on his feet, once more searching for a way out of the building. There just wasn't a way.

He slept at last, curled up under the thin ragged blanket that was left for him. He didn't hear the door unlock and then squeak open or the man who dropped a bag of food on the floor for him. The man shook his head. He had no idea why Arlyn was there but he wasn't sure that he wanted to be part of kidnapping. And that was exactly what it was.

The next morning, Arlyn's eyes opened and he searched for whoever it was that had been in the room with him overnight. He was alone. His eyes looked up and he gave a small smile. God was there, to protect him and to comfort him. Arlyn was convinced of that.

On his feet, Arlyn walked the building, finding the bag of food on the floor. He stared down at it and then reached to pick it up, opening it to find sandwiches and apples. He sighed. This would be his meal, he decided, knowing that he needed to eat but reluctant to do so.

Arlyn sat on the bunk again, his thoughts muddled. He waited for whoever it was who had kidnapped him to appear, but no one did. Day turned into night and then into another day. Arlyn continued to wait, sure that whoever it was would appear at some point. He slept at last, unable to keep his eyes open.

The man who had brought the original bag of food snuck towards the building, looking over his shoulders to determine if he was being followed. He wasn't. He knew that the other men were either drunk or high on drugs and that suited him just fine. He reached to unlock the door, having already oiled the hinges on a trip to check on Arlyn. He reached to draw Arlyn to his feet, despite the fact that Arlyn was protesting and not really awake.

Walking away from the farm, the man kept Arlyn on his feet by his grip on Arlyn's arm. He walked them for what seemed miles until morning had broken. At that point, they were near Arlyn's home. The man drew Arlyn into the shadows of a building and waited. He saw the cars passing by and knew that the men had discovered Arlyn's disappearance and were looking for him.

Arlyn had dropped to the ground, almost too tired to stand. He was hurting in spirit and body and wasn't sure where he exactly was. He was drawn to his feet again and with a hand on his back directed to his home. The man reached for Arlyn's keys and unlocked the back door, shoving Arlyn inside and then dropping the keys on the counter. He walked away, heading for where he wasn't sure. All he knew was that he had helped out someone and that he now needed to head from Grasspoint in order to stay alive.

Chapter 36

Arlyn came back to the present time, eyeing Joe as he did so. He had no idea who the men where, he stated, or why. There had been no contact with anyone, other than the man who had seemed to help him. He had been asked for nothing and told nothing.

Joe was listening carefully, a frown on his face.

"Do you know where you were?" Joe looked up as Arlyn did not respond.

"I have no idea, Joe. I really don't. I was blindfolded when I was taken there. And when the man helped me, I was just too out of it. I was in a fog. I know that we seemed to walk forever. And it seemed that it was a farm." Arlyn's face paled. "I think I know who it is." He said a name, causing Joe to pause in what he was doing to stare at Arlyn.

Skylor had been listening closely, her eyes darting from Arlyn to Joe and back again.

"Who is this person?" Skylor's voice broke through the silence that had followed the dropping of the name.

"He's someone who is high in the agricultural industry here in town. He puts on a good front but there have been rumours about him." Arlyn rubbed at his face again, something that he seemed to be doing a lot lately. "We need to find him and bring him down, Joe. He would have the resources and contacts for black market trading in endangered species. If I remember correctly, that's where some of the endangered hawks have their habitat."

Joe was nodding. They would need to do just that. Only he had no idea how to do that or who to reach out to.

"You have some ideas?" Joe asked the obvious question.

"I will have. I have some but for now, I need to sleep." Arlyn rose and headed for his bedroom, shutting the door quietly behind him before he simply crawled under the covers and slept.

Skylor stared after him before she turned to Joe. Joe was staring towards the hallway, a thoughtful look on his face.

"Joe? How do we do this? It's not over for Arlyn. It won't be until you find and arrest that man." Skylor stared at him, not backing down. This was new for her, Joe knew, and part of her healing process.

"No, it's not over for Arlyn. This is where it gets much more dangerous for Arlyn. And also for you. That man will go after you to get to Arlyn. We know that. I know that we have your father or the man who called himself your father in custody. That part is over, we think."

"You think? Then you're not sure. Someone was behind him, weren't they?" Skylor sighed, thinking that she had done that way too often.

"That's the consensus that we seem to have come to. I won't ask if you know who. I doubt that you will." Joe paused, a frown on his face. "Who watched you when you were young?"

Skylor shrugged. That was not something that she had ever really thought about.

"No one. He would just lock me in a room with food and water and leave me there until he decided to return. I learned not to ask for anything. He would beat me if I did, even as a toddler." Skylor was matter of fact in her words.

Joe was horrified at that. He has suspected something along those lines but to have it confirmed? He wanted the men responsible for that just as much as he wanted the man responsible for the black market trade in endangered birds. Arlyn and Skylor were still in danger and he had no way of knowing when or if they would ever be safe.

Skylor tidied away the remnants and dishes from their meal before she paced around the kitchen. She glanced at the clock and then headed for the living room. She had no keys to lock up the house and wouldn't leave it unlocked. She reached for a blanket and curled up on the couch. Skylor didn't sleep but instead kept watch over the night. She finally slept as dawn was breaking through the clouds that covered the eastern sky.

Arlyn was on his feet and heading for the rest of the house. He was afraid that someone who wanted to harm him was in his house. He paused as he reached the living room, seeing a low light on that he didn't remember leaving on. He walked towards the couch, a soft smile lighting his face as he saw Skylor still sleeping. She had kept watch for him overnight, allowing him to sleep in peace.

Arlyn touched her hair lightly with a forefinger, his love for her evident on his face. He walked away from her, heading for his office. He reached to wake up his computer and then to read through his emails. He paused at one, his face going white and then stern before he forwarded it on to Joe. He had no idea what that person wanted or what he had that they thought he had. He had nothing that could be used on the black market. His face paled even more as he realized what they wanted. They wanted his knowledge of the area and where the endangered birds were. They would use him to trap the birds, making sure that he became part of their crimes.

On his feet, Arlyn paced before he headed back to the living room. He found a chair where he could watch Skylor sleep, knowing that she was in deep danger as well. He had no idea that the man who called himself her father had been arrested but that there were others out there trying to kidnap her.

Skylor roused slowly, her eyes opening to a room that was not hers. She sat up abruptly, shoving aside the blanket. She was ready to jump to her feet and run when she saw Arlyn sitting nearby, his eyes closed.

"Arlyn?" Skylor spoke quietly, just loud enough to rouse him.

"Skylor? You're here? You didn't go home last night." Arlyn watched her closely.

"No, I didn't. I couldn't. You needed someone with you." Skylor yawned. "Did you call your family?"

"I sent off a text when I got home. They're to come here this morning." Arlyn was disturbed at how much their lives had been disturbed.

"They are?" Skylor was on her feet, heading for her apartment. She needed to change to clean clothes before she was back up at Arlyn's, searching the kitchen for food.

Arlyn watched her for a moment before he approached her and stopped her movements. He wrapped her into his arms and then kissed her.

"Marry me, Skylor?" Arlyn simply hugged her tighter.

"Arlyn? Marry you? Are you sure?" Skylor struggled to lean back and look up at him, not sure of his words or if he was sure of what he had said.

"I am, Skylor. I just don't know if you're ready for that." Arlyn kissed her again before he stepped back. "Pray it over, Skylor. And then we'll talk. For now, we need to eat." He reached to help prepare a simple breakfast.

His brothers stared at him in shock as he told them what had happened. He knew that his parents and aunt were standing behind him, listening as well.

"That happened? That doesn't make sense, Arlyn." Briar paced away from his brother, leaving Cayce to stare at him.

<hr>

"It did, Briar. It really did. I just don't know who it is that is behind all this. And I hear that Skylor's father has been arrested but it's not over for her."

"No, it's not." Ardan spoke, drawing his sons' attention to him. "And we need to end it somehow."

Chapter 37

Arlyn approached his father hours later. They had been working through all the information that they had but felt that there was something that was missing in all of it. They had no idea what or who it was.

"Dad? What are we missing? I know that there's something missing." Arlyn sat beside his father, handing over his notes.

"We are missing something, son." Ardan studied his son, seeing the strain and stress that the last few days had left on his face. "Listen to me and then talk to me. If someone wants to send black market material out of the country, how would you do it?"

Arlyn thought through the process of how he would send out black market material. He nodded, knowing that his father had asked the question that they had all been dancing around.

"How to send it out? Find a company or courier company that transports out of the country. And there are a number here who do that. It can be done without anyone knowing anything about it. The material can be hidden in packages. Unless someone is suspicious of a package, search it, or someone has called the authorities to warn them, it would not be found."

Ardan was nodding. They now had to look for that as well. He sent off a swift text to Joe, who stared at his message and sighed. They had just found another avenue to investigate. He would check in with them later. At the moment, he was due at another crime scene.

Briar had looked up as the two men were speaking and then looked down at the paperwork that Emma had sent. She had found the link for them. He had no idea how she had done that. No one, not even Emma herself, could explain it.

"Dad? Read this." Briar was on his feet, heading for his father and Arlyn to hand over the papers that he held. "This is the connection."

Ardan stared at his son and then down at the paperwork. He drew in a deep breath. Briar had been right. This was the connection.

"When did you find this?" Arlyn had been reading over his father's shoulder.

"I didn't. Emma did and sent it on yesterday, I think it was." Briar was dismayed. "It's been sitting there for twenty-four hours."

"We didn't know, son." Ardan looked around as everyone in the room seemed to be staring at him. "Emma found the person who's behind the transportation of the contraband. Now, we just need to prove it."

"And we will." Cayce reached for the papers, reading through them. "He's out of town right now, did you know that? Very convenient, I would say."

"He is?" Skylor approached the men, reaching for the papers in turn. She frowned. "I don't know this man. How does he connect to Smith?"

They all stared at Skylor. That was something that none of them had thought of. Anna reached for another stack of papers that she had just set to one side. She drew in a deep breath. Skylor had asked the correct question. Anna was on her feet and reaching for a maker. She began to write out names on a clear piece of paper. The rest of them in the room gathered around her, Skylor tight to her side.

Skylor read the names, a frown on her face. Somehow, they seemed familiar. Then she remembered what had happened about a year or so previous. She had come upon a list of names in the kitchen of the house where she had been held captive. These names were on them.

"I know those names. I found a list a year ago. I wasn't to see them. I tried to memorize them before I was locked away again." Skylor drew in a deep breath. "I did this, didn't I?"

"No, you didn't. Smith did." Arlyn's arms held her as she almost wept in defeat. "He did it. Now that we have the names, we can pass them on to whoever it is that we need to." He looked around as the door bell rang. "Were we expecting anyone?"

"Not that I know of." Cayce headed for the door, standing back to let Joe enter. "Joe?"

"Where are they?" Joe's words were almost bit out, causing Cayce to stare at him. "Arlyn? Skylor? Where are they?"

"In the office. Why?"

"There have been developments that we need to discuss." Joe headed that way, anger almost sparking from him.

Cayce followed him, frowning at his words. He watched as Joe stood and watched Arlyn and Skylor as they discussed the newest developments with Anna and Briar.

Skylor looked around at last, seeing Joe. She made her way to him, frowning at him.

"Joe? You're troubled?"

"I am, Skylor. I am. We need to find a way to keep you and Arlyn safe. And I don't know that we can." Joe sighed. "We need to talk, Skylor. Smith is dead. He tried to escape as he was being taken into court for a bail hearing. No, it wasn't one of our people who shot him. It was a sniper and that sniper has disappeared."

Skylor stared at him in shock. To hear that Smith was dead and in such a violent manner was not what she expected to hear. She began to shake as she realized that she no longer had to face him.

Arlyn had been watching her and was at her side, wrapping her into his arms. He had no idea what Joe had just told her but obviously something had happened. All he could do was pray for his lady.

"Joe?" Arlyn turned to his friend. "What did you just tell her?"

"Smith is dead. He was taken down by a sniper. And no, we don't have the sniper in custody." Joe was frustrated at that.

"I see." Arlyn tilted his head to watch Skylor. "That takes away one area that we need to watch for, but it opens up something else, doesn't it? How do we stay safe, Joe? We can't stay at home. I have to be out in the field. And Skylor needs to be able to move around freely. She has been held captive for far too many years."

Chapter 38

Arlyn paced his back yard late that afternoon. Everyone had left, not wanting to but they all had commitments that they needed to be at. He knew that Skylor had planted herself on the back steps, her eyes watching his every movement. She didn't want to let him out of her sight, afraid that he would disappear once more and this time not to come home, at least not alive.

He sighed. There was just so much uncertainty about what they knew and what they didn't know. He walked back towards Skylor, sitting beside her. His arm wrapped around her, drawing her close to his side.

"Arlyn? Where do we go from here? I need to leave. Smith isn't out there now and I have the freedom to do that." Skylor was sober as she spoke. She didn't want to leave but knew that she had to.

"I don't want you to leave, not ever. I want to marry you, Skylor, and spend what time that God gives us with you." Arlyn bit at his lip. He hadn't meant to say that so soon.

Skylor stared at the field in front of her. She wondered that he had stated that. She was not marrying material. She was too damaged. Then, she sighed. God knew her worth and would heal her. She just wasn't expecting healing. Not any more. That hope had been destroyed many years ago.

"I can't stay, Arlyn. You need someone better and more whole than me."

"No, you're the picture of the lady who I've dreamed about for years. Just think about it." Arlyn was on his feet, drawing her upright. "Let's go out for a meal. I don't feel like cooking. Besides, we need to be out and about to draw those people out."

"I know. That's what I'm afraid of, Arlyn. I'm afraid that you will be killed." Skylor didn't listen to her words. She was sharing her heart with him. Arlyn studied her and then simply hugged her.

Late that night, men moved in around Arlyn's home. They planted themselves where they could watch the house and then take Arlyn captive once more. Their eyes sought Skylor's windows and knew that they would need to take her captive to ensure that Arlyn cooperated with them. They just didn't know how that would happen.

Skylor stepped out of her apartment the next morning and then headed to the office. Unlocking the door, she stepped into the room and then locked the door behind her. She didn't see the men rushing to capture her. They were frustrated by the locked door. The men slunk away and back to where they remained hidden. There would have to be a chance to take them.

Arlyn watched Skylor as she worked away, knowing that she was struggling to concentrate and then to think through what she needed to do. It was a difficult balance that he had to walk with her, not wanting to smother her but also wanting to help her out as much as he could.

Skylor looked up, jumping as she saw Arlyn watching her. She frowned at him before her attention went back to the mail that she was sorting through. She glanced up briefly as Arlyn walked by her and to his own desk.

Silence reigned in the room as the couple worked away. Arlyn sat back at last, a frown on his face. He was on his feet, heading for the filing cabinet and then searching through it for the folder he needed. He opened it when he found it, drawing in a deep breath. Here was part of the answer for what he was facing. Arlyn had forgotten about these documents until now. He sighed. He would need to send them on to Joe. He turned as he felt a hand on his arm.

Skylor had reached out numerous times before she cautiously laid a hand on his arm. She reached then for the folder, reading through it, puzzled at what she was reading.

"Arlyn? What is this?"

"This? This information may well solve what I'm going through. It's from a few years ago, unfortunately. I need to get it to Joe." He thought for a moment before he was at Skylor's desk, laying each piece of paper out and then reaching for his phone, intent on taking the photos that he needed of the papers. He paused as once more Skylor's hand rested on his arm.

"Talk to me, Arlyn. Tell me what you are doing." Skylor had no idea what he was up to.

"I'm taking pictures of the pages." Arlyn held up his phone so that she could see it. "There is a camera on the phone. Once I take the pictures, then I can either send them as an email or a text message." He studied her. "This is all so new to you."

"It is. I feel like an infant just learning how to walk." Skylor blinked rapidly, trying to control her emotions. "Go on, Arlyn. Let me see how you do it."

Arlyn nodded and then set about doing exactly what he had told her. He watched Skylor as he did so, seeing the interest on her face. He decided then that they had been selling Skylor short and they needed to do better. He reached to hug her, finding her hugging him back. That seemed to be such a small gesture but he knew that she was putting herself out of her comfort zone.

"What happens now?" Skylor walked around the office, studying everything. She frowned. "Arlyn? What is this?"

"What's what?" Arlyn roused from his thoughts and turned towards Skylor. "What did you find?"

"This? I don't remember it being here yesterday." She pointed at a stuffed bird. "It doesn't look like Briar's work."

Arlyn paled, his hand reached for the bird. It was sloppily done and he would hazard a guess that it was not by a trained taxidermist. He ran for the door, throwing the bird as far from him as he could before he slammed the door and then grabbed for Skylor. He shoved her to the floor, covering her with his body.

The shock from the exploding bird shook the building, Skylor screamed even as she hid her face in

---

her arms. Arlyn's hand kept her on the floor as he sat up, shaken by what had happened.

Joe walked towards Arlyn, shaking his head. This was not what he had expected to hear.

"What bird was it?" Joe's question caught at Arlyn's attention.

"A stuffed cardinal. I have no idea when it was placed in there. Skylor found it. If she hadn't, we likely wouldn't be here." Arlyn was angry, more angry than he had been. This had been just too close for them.

Chapter 39

Joe stared at Arlyn's open office door in frustration. It was obviously broken in and the couple were nowhere in sight. He turned as he heard a voice calling to him and walked towards a crime scene tech.

"No one there?" Phil looked past him.

"No, they're gone. I had an email from Arlyn an hour ago. Now this." Joe was frustrated but also highly worried. The word on the street that had reached him was that the couple were to disappear that day. And it seemed as if that word was correct.

Phil shook his head. He was acquainted with the Koyle brothers from school and thought highly of them.

"Where are they?" He walked towards the office to being processing the scene. This was not what he had expected.

Joe walked around the yard and then tried the house doors. They were locked tightly. The only open door was the office one. He returned to enter the office, looking around. Nothing seemed to be disturbed and that worried him. How did the manage to disappear?

Ardan stepped back from his front door two hours later, a worried look on his face that Joe had appeared on his doorstep.

"Joe? I don't like it that you're here."

"I don't like it either. Have you seen either Arlyn or Skylor today?" Joe watched keenly as Ardan shook his head.

"No, we haven't. We hadn't expected to. Why?" Bessie had appeared, a worried look suddenly on her face.

"I was just at his office. The door has been broken in and Arlyn and Skylor are not there." Joe gave a deep sigh. "I was hoping that they were here." He looked past the older couple to see Briar and Cayce watching him.

"They've got them, have they?" Arden had been afraid of that. "Okay. Then, you need to come in and see what the boys have discovered. It may help. Samuel, Simon, and Blackie have sent on information as has Emma. Emma also said that her husband and his security team were heading this way. She didn't say why."

Abe walked toward Cayce and Briar, finding them outside of Arlyn's office, watching the activity that was still going on. He sighed to himself. Emma had received word that there was a contract out on both of the couple and he had rushed his team there. It looked suspiciously as if they were too late.

"Briar? Cayce?" Abe's voice brought their attention to him. His team walked behind him, their heads in motion as they monitored the onlookers and then looked past them for anyone who looked suspicious.

"Abe? You're here?" Briar shook his head. "They're not here, Abe. They disappeared."

"That's what Emma was afraid of. She sent us here, praying that we were in time." Abe looked past the brothers. "What do you know?"

"Not a whole lot. Joe stated that Skylor had a stuffed bird in the office and Arlyn realized there was an issue with it. He pitched it out into the yard and it exploded. Sometime between when he sent a message to Joe and when Joe arrived, they were taken from here. The office door has been broken into." Cayce's voice held his deep worry for brother and his lady.

Abe shared a look with his business partner and good friend, Murphy. This is not what they had wanted. Murphy nodded and walked away, his phone out to call Emma. Nathaniel and Luke walked with him, knowing that they would act at some point. For now, they would monitor the area.

Abe walked back towards his team, worried about the couple, and unable to relieve the worry of the two brothers. He had not spoken to Joe, not wishing to disturb the investigation. He made plans to catch up with him later, if possible.

"Abe?" Murphy pocketed his phone. "Emma has an address. It's just outside of town." He shot a look towards Joe, finding that man watching the team. "She's speaking with the police services who enforce that area. She said for us to head that way and that we would be met."

Abe nodded before walking rapidly to their van. The team disappeared from sight, leaving those watching them to exchange looks with one another and then turn their attention back to the tasks at hand.

———

Ardan and Bessie turned at the boys entered their home, their aunt following them. They hugged each other before finding their seats in the office and spending time in prayer. They were well aware that was the only thing that they could do at present. God was in control and had the couple in His care. He was the One who would free them. They just might not like how they were freed.

Abe stood for a moment, eyeing the house in front of him. Emma had confirmed the address with the police services and the emergency task force for that service were standing with them. The discussion was which team would go in.

Abe finally made a move towards the house, the ETF group with them. The ETF team was prepared to go in first, with Abe following them. It was not what Abe wanted but what he was willing to work with.

The doorknob turned under the ETF's leader hand which surprised them. They burst into the house, shouting that the police were there and that whoever was there needed to surrender. There was silence in the house as the police searched.

Abe and his team followed, searching themselves. Abe paused for a moment to check a text from Emma and then pointed to the outside. His team ran with him, heading for the outside and then towards a mound of dirt that was not that far from the house. They slowed their steps, coming to a halt in front of a door. Luke reached with the bolt cutters that he had carried, cutting through the padlock and pulling the door open. It creaked as it slid towards them, dust and cobwebs flying through the air.

Murphy, Joseph, and Matt headed down into the darkness, the other five watching for any danger. A large flashlight lit the room, shining in Arlyn's and Skylor's eyes as they stood with their backs to the dirt wall. They moved forward on a run as Matt pointed towards the door. They were rushed from there and towards the van waiting for them. The ETF leader appeared, surprised to see the couple before he nodded. He motioned to a patrol officer to lead the van away from the site. There would be time to interrogate the couple once they were safe.

Chapter 40

Arlyn refused to let go of Skylor, drawing looks from Abe's team. They knew what it was like to be in danger and have their ladies in danger. They had all gone through what they called adventures and had faced life-and-death circumstances.

Abe shifted on his seat to study the couple, a slight smile on his face. Murphy had reached out to Emma and then Joe. Joe had been surprised and delighted that the couple was safe. He only asked that Abe's team find somewhere to keep them safe until he could reach them.

"Arlyn? Are you two okay? Do you need to see any emergency services?" Abe's voice was quiet but tight as he controlled his emotions.

"We're fine. They just locked us up. They threatened Skylor to get me to cooperate. And it worked." Arlyn was angry. They had been in danger once more, with Skylor threatened. He had recognized the men who had taken them away from his office and that had worried him. He knew who they worked for.

"You know who they are." Joseph spoke up. "And you want to bring them down."

"I do. And I want to be there when he is taken down." Arlyn looked down at Skylor as she made a motion. "Skylor?"

"No, you don't need to be there for justice to be done, Arlyn. You want to be and that is something different." Skylor was adamant that Arlyn would not be there. He had to leave it to the authorities. God would bring justice for them, of that she was certain.

"No? I want to be the one, Skylor." Arlyn sighed, his hand tightening on hers. "I know that I can't bring justice for us. Others have to do that." He slid from the van, reaching for her hand and tugging her out as well. "Abe? Where are we to go?"

"For now, we'll lock you into that building behind us. Once Joe has made contact with us, then we'll see about getting you back home. And yes, we have reached out to your family, Arlyn, and they are aware that you two are safe." Abe walked away to make a phone call. He felt the threat that was there and was unsettled. He didn't think it was over for the couple but he had no way of knowing that for sure.

A sudden popping sound had Abe's team reacting. Ian took Arlyn to the ground with a hand on his back to keep him down. Murphy reacted in the same way with Skylor. He frowned for a moment as something seemed off with her but he wasn't able to even process that thought.

A patrol officer had his weapon out and was reacting. One shot took down the assailant. Four officers raced towards him, one dropping to the ground beside the man. He was on his feet, shaking his head. The assassin had passed on to meet God and would be not judged by them.

Abe's team stood from where they had dropped to the ground, looking around. Murphy reached to help Skylor to her feet before he was yelling for Matt, their paramedic. Matt was on his knees beside her, helping

Murphy roll her to her back. They drew in their breath sharply before Nathaniel was reaching for the first-aid kit and dropping it beside him. Skylor had been hit in the abdomen. It looked bad, Matt decided, as he worked frantically to stem the flow of blood. Ian's arm around Arlyn's shoulder kept that man just out of reach of Skylor. Arlyn was horrified that she had been shot.

Abe was angry. This should not have happened. They should have been safe here and hadn't been. Someone had leaked their location and he was determined to find out just who it had been.

Joe ran towards the group, his car door slamming behind him. He had not been prepared to hear that Skylor had been shot. He stopped short of where the paramedics were working on Skylor. Matt had stepped back, Micah pouring water over his hands to try and remove the blood. Joe walked towards Abe.

"Abe? What happened?"

"An assassin. We just didn't see him. None of us did. How did he know where we were?" Abe bit out his words, anger very much evident.

Joe was shocked but also angered. He paced away from Abe and headed for the paramedics, standing at the back of the rig as they settled Skylor. He didn't like the look on their faces. He waved a patrol officer over and then sent him ahead of the rig to rush Skylor in. He then turned to Arlyn, seeing that man was in shock.

Abe managed to get Arlyn back into their van before they drove away. He was still fighting mad, as they say, worried about Skylor and Arlyn, but determined to find out why and who. And that Emma was working on, she had said.

Milling around the hospital, Abe's team was particularly watchful. It was rare that someone had been hurt on their watch and each man took it personally. They watched Arlyn and his family as they sat and waited for word on Skylor.

The physician finally stood back from Skylor's stretcher. He breathed a sigh of relief, knowing that the wound looked much worse than it was. Sure, she would need surgery but the bullet had missed anything vital. It had cut through the muscle. He pondered that for a moment and then nodded. She was on the move when she was hit, just by the angle. He would find the young man who had protected her and thank him.

Late that evening, Arlyn stood beside Skylor's hospital bed, her hand in his. She was starting to rouse. He had been standing there for a long time, willing her to awaken but at the same time praying for healing. He had been thankful that the bullet had not done more damage than it had, given the amount of blood that flowed from her. Arlyn had been terrified that she would die before he had a chance to spend a lifetime with her.

Skylor stirred restlessly, her hand reaching for her side. She heard Arlyn's soft prayers for her and struggled to open her eyes.

"Arlyn? Are you there?" Her voice was just above a whisper.

"I am, my love. God is good. You weren't killed, and we're free once more." He reached to drop a kiss on her forehead. "And here is Joe."

Joe walked towards them, his shoes quiet on the floor. He was exhausted, having spent the hours between the shooting and now tracking down the culprits and other victims. It was a huge mess, he decided, but as of now, they had the people behind the attacks of Arlyn and behind the black market trade in the endangered birds.

"Joe? Is it over? I want this over." Skylor yawned and then slept, not seeing the smiles on the men's faces.

"It's over, Skylor. It's over. And we will meet in a few days, Arlyn, to let you all know the outcome of the investigation."

"It's over?" Arlyn stared at his friend and the investigator responsible for their case.

"It is, Arlyn. It finally is. We have work to do now to wrap up the investigation and then turn everything over to the crown attorney for them to decide charges. I'll leave an officer at the door for the night." Joe walked away, nodding at the family who were still in the waiting room and heading for the outdoors. He stood in the cool night air, turning his face up to the stars and moon shining so brightly down on him. His eyes closed as a prayer of thanks and praise raised to the God who had brought justice to his friends.

Chapter 41

A week later, Skylor curled up on the couch in Arlyn's living room, snuggling close to him. This was a change for her. Three weeks ago, she would not have done that, feeling too restricted by her past. What she had gone through had changed that, freeing her to find love at last, the love that she had longed and prayed for. She had opened her heart to love and found Arlyn just walking right in.

Arlyn's arm tightened around Skylor as he watched his family gathering in the room. Joe was there, laughing with Cayce as Briar found a seat on the couch beside Skylor. Briar just grinned at his brother before he looked at Skylor. He nodded to himself. They were the perfect couple, he decided.

Ardan's voice could be heard over the other voices, calling everyone to quiet and then to a time of prayer. They could feel the presence of God in the room, humbled before Him.

Joe looked up at last, his eyes on Arlyn and Skylor. They were focused on him, waiting for him to speak. There was a peace about them that he didn't see often but knew that it came from God. He was the only One who could give that peace.

"Joe? What can you tell us?" Arlyn broke the silence in the room, asking the question that everyone there wanted to be the one to ask.

"What can I tell you?" Joe drew in a deep breath. "First, I am glad and thankful that you both are alive and relatively healthy. I know that you will never be the people that you were before. Skylor, you are now free of the man who abused you for your whole life. I am thankful for that. God has plans for you that He will work out. Trust Him to do that."

"Who was it, Joe? Who did this to us?" Arlyn had to tamp down the anger that could still swell within him.

"Who was it? Who did this to you?" At Arlyn's nod, Joe studied each one of the others in the room, seeing the anticipation on their faces. "It was Woodrow Thomson."

"Thomson?" Arlyn was shocked at that. "Him? And he's so into saving the endangered species of any sort."

"That's correct. He had the perfect opportunity to find out about any endangered species, including your birds. He knew where they had their habitats. There is a big black market for any endangered specie, not just here in Canada but world wide. He used your knowledge at times to find your birds and trap them. He was a user of anyone who he felt would serve him and no one was the wiser." Joe hesitated for a moment. "Everything that happened to you, Arlyn, was at his orders. And he owned the courier company that shipped the specimens."

Arlyn drew in a deep breath. He had not been prepared to hear that.

"What about Skylor? That shooting?" Ardan spoke up.

"The shooting? That was Smith's doing. He had arranged that if he was ever arrested, Skylor was to be killed in the worst way possible, a shooting." Joe looked towards Skylor, not seeing the shame or defeat that he expected to see in her. "I am sorry to say, Skylor, that he was your father. Emma has gone back over what she had been told and found that she had been lied to very badly. The couple who pretended to be your parents had the right talk and the right documents. Smith arranged for that. From what we can find out, he killed your mother in a drunken rage when you were born. He refused to let her deliver in the hospital. He put out word that you both died in an accident and not one person questioned him. He had a vile black heart. He used the name of Smith although Sage was his real last name."

"He did and I bore the brunt of that." Skylor was saddened. She already knew that her mother had been killed. Blackie and Samuel had visited her a few days before just to confirm that with her. "Blackie told me that, Joe, so it's not a surprise. I think I always knew that. At least now, I can live my life without fear. And so can Arlyn. From what I have read, there is a large amount of money to be made in the black market. You have taken away one person or group of people who were involved in that. Thank you. God has used you to keep justice in this world. I also know that there was no inheritance. That was a rumour that he started. It's okay. God has the riches that I need."

Joe nodded, knowing what she wasn't saying. He rose at last, walking away to another crime scene. He prayed for his friends, knowing that God had had them in His hands and had brought justice to the culprits for them.

Skylor moved around Arlyn's home later that day. The family had all left, hugging her and welcoming her to the family. She had frowned at their smiles before shaking her head. That wasn't about to happen, she decided. Arlyn had not said anything more than what he had.

Arlyn appeared beside her, wrapping her into his arms, a kiss to her temple. She hugged him back, feeling some freedom in doing that. It would take a lot of prayers and work on her part to overcome her past.

"Okay, sweetheart?" Arlyn laid his head on hers.

"I am, thank you, Arlyn. And you?" She felt his head nodding against her.

"I want to take you out for a real meal, sweetheart. Dress up and everything. I know that you have never done that but I would really like to see you all gussied up." He laughed down at the look on her face. "I love you, Skylor, and would love to marry you."

Skylor stared up at the tall man staring down at her before she simply reached to hug him.

"I love you too, Arlyn. I never thought that I would ever feel this way. That was beaten down so far in me. You have helped me to recover my life. You and God."

"You're right. God has done that and will continue to do that. You are a free lady, someone who I really love." He kissed her at that point. He spoke once more. "God was there for us, protecting us, covering us with His hand, and using us to bring people to justice. It's what He does."

"He does. I just wish it hadn't been so hard." Her hand rested on her side. "I could have done without being shot." She frowned as he grinned. "It's not funny."

"No, it's not but that comment is just so you. For now, head on home, sweetheart. We're not working tomorrow, so plan on spending it out in the open, just the two of us and some birds if we can find them."

Skylor nodded, her face glowing before she walked away. She was loved and loved in return. God had been gracious, she decided, providing rescue and freedom for her and justice for both Arlyn and herself.

A year later, Skylor was on the hunt for her husband of six months. He was not in the house or his office. She stood, hands on her hips, before a smile broke out on her face and she ran for the back yard and then to the trees that lined the field behind them.

Arlyn turned as he heard the running footsteps, his arms open to welcome his bride. He kissed her and then kissed her again. They were deeply in love with each other, content that God had worked out His best for them.

"Happy, sweetheart?" Arlyn grinned at her.

"I am. What are you up to?" Skylor didn't move from his arms.

"This. There's a pair of woodpeckers in this tree. And there are just so many other species here. I am so glad that we were able to protect the endangered ones."

"I am too." Skylor stared up at the sky. "It was coming up to night, twilight the time of day that she seemed to have come to love best. "We went through so much, not as much as others, but it was still dangerous for us."

"It was. I am so glad that we came through everything. I was so worried at one point that we would be killed." Arlyn turned them to walk back towards the house. They were due to have supper with the family soon but he didn't want to walk away from the serenity in their back yard.

"God was indeed gracious. He kept justice for us and for others. Joe spoke to me earlier today about how many species that were endangered because of that man." Skylor refused to speak the man's name.

"There were and other people were threatened as well." Arlyn paused as they reached the steps. "Are you okay working in the office? I mean, is there something else that you would like to do?"

Skylor shook her head. She loved the work that Arlyn was involved in and was doing her best to help out. She was in school on line to learn more about it and was taking courses towards an administration diploma. She was loved and happy.

"No, I'm okay working there. My life is full for now." Skylor looked up at Arlyn, a frown momentarily on her face. "Why would you ask?"

"I just want you to be where you want to be. You lost that freedom for so many years that I don't want you not to be free to do what you want to do." Arlyn kissed her again before turning her to the house, walking through it and locking the doors after them. "Mom's expecting us for dinner."

"I know. Your parents are just so sweet as is your aunt. Now, your brothers? That's a different story." Her face lit up with laughter as Arlyn laughed.

"I know what you mean, sweetheart, but you're the sister that they never had." Arlyn stopped on the front sidewalk, a sudden thought of his brothers facing danger wafting through him. "You bring just what we need in the family. God prepared this path for you before time began."

"He did at that." Skylor was content to stand with her groom and meditate on God.

Thank you for picking up the story of Arlyn and Skylor. I knew that I wanted Arlyn to be an ornithologist but I had no idea of the life that Skylor had lived or that she would have been raised in an abusive family. That is how the characters develop in my novels. And I had no idea that endangered bird species would be central to the story.

God is there. He is there in each aspect of our lives. He brings justice to those who need to have justice. And He never ever leaves us or turns His back on us. That is a promise that He keeps.

And as usual, other characters turn up from their stories. Blackie and Simon's stories are in *Mistletoe Treasures*. Abe and his team are in *His Guardians*. Rachel's story is *The* Anchor and Gideon's is *The* Haven, part of *The Haven of* Rest series. Abe usually shows up a lot earlier in the story. This time it was Blackie, Simon, and Samuel took over that role. My characters just can't stay in their own stories. They have to walk back and forth.

The concept of the brothers being triplets was not planned either. It was only after I started writing that they decided that was what they were. My characters don't share very readily at times about their stories even though I talk to them and ask them what their stories are.

Birds have been a fascination for me all my life. As a child, I spent the first twelve years of my life being raised on a five acre plot of land in the country.

My mother loved birds and passed that love onto my sister and myself. By the time that we left that farm, we had tracked at least sixty different species of birds. Those were days that I wish I could go back to.

As to the little gray tabby kitty? A friend and the breeder of my Shelties found a little gray tabby, about eight weeks old, in the middle of a highway and risked her life to rescue her. I took her in and called her Ceilidh (Kayleigh), as reference to the Irish heritage on my Mom's side. I unfortunately lost her when she was not quite four as she was sick. I miss this kitty so much, a kitty who was so convinced that she was a Sheltie and not a cat at all.

May God bless you on your walk with Him.

Ronna

www.ingramcontent.com/pod-product-compliance
Lightning Source LLC
Chambersburg PA
CBHW060407310726

48976CB00003B/968